I Agree with you

THE BLOOD OF IRON EYES

In Arizona territory, bounty hunter Iron Eyes adds another outlaw to his tally and heads for the town of Hope to collect his reward money. Unfortunately, the outlaw had worked for Brewster Fontaine, who pretty much owns the whole town — including the bank ... Fontaine orders his hired guns to kill Iron Eyes the moment he leaves the bank. But Iron Eyes is no ordinary bounty hunter and will wage war no matter how many guns he must face.

Books by Rory Black
in the Linford Western Library:

THE FURY OF IRON EYES
THE WRATH OF IRON EYES
THE CURSE OF IRON EYES
THE SPIRIT OF IRON EYES
THE GHOST OF IRON EYES
IRON EYES MUST DIE

RORY BLACK

THE BLOOD OF IRON EYES

Complete and Unabridged

LINFORD
Leicester

First published in Great Britain in 2006 by
Robert Hale Limited
London

First Linford Edition
published 2007
by arrangement with
Robert Hale Limited
London

The moral right of the author
has been asserted

British Library CIP Data

Black, Rory
    The blood of Iron Eyes.—Large print ed.—
Linford western library
    1. Western stories
    2. Large type books
    I. Title
    823.9'14 [F]
    788 3319
    ISBN 978–1–84617–659–3

Published by
F. A. Thorpe (Publishing)
Anstey, Leicestershire

Set by Words & Graphics Ltd.
Anstey, Leicestershire
Printed and bound in Great Britain by
T. J. International Ltd., Padstow, Cornwall

This book is printed on acid-free paper

Dedicated to my friend,
Richard Gordon.
Film Producer/Director
and gentleman.

1

There was a chilling silence throughout the dense woodland which overlooked a vast rolling range bathed in moonlight far below. Only the sound of the horse's hoofs as the exhausted animal negotiated the brittle ground between an ocean of tall pines echoed through the silent terrain. It was as if every living creature that occupied the tree-covered slopes instinctively sensed that there was someone deadly moving through their territory. The aroma of stale killings hung on the horseman and warned them of the lethal presence of a hunter in their midst.

A hunter unlike most of his bloody profession. A man who was far more deadly than any who had ridden through this place before. Yet this awesome rider had ceased to hunt mere animals long ago. He had turned his unequalled skills to a prey far more profitable.

Wanted men drew far greater prizes.

Sweat dripped from the mane of long, limp, black hair over his left hand, which gripped the reins tightly. His small bullet-coloured eyes, set amid a face covered with countless brutal scars, burned at the moonlit trail ahead. He knew that he was not the first to have ridden this way during the previous few hours.

Broken branches and a million other clues told the skilled hunter that the outlaw he had trailed for more than a week had been this way only a short time ahead of him.

Few others would have spotted the small rocks on the ground which had been moved as Daniel Kane rode through this remote woodland, trying to flee the man on his tail. Yet the rider who had turned his hunting skills from animals to men long before his prey had even been born, knew he was getting closer with every beat of his cold heart.

Now he was so close, he could actually smell Kane!

His unmatched prowess had become legendary in the minds of both the good and the bad men who roamed the Wild West. Hated and feared equally by them all, the bounty hunter had achieved almost mythical infamy.

For to have this bounty hunter on your trail was as good as being certified dead. This was a man who did not know the meaning of the word 'quit'. Some said that he could not be killed for he was not truly alive. Many believed that he was a ghost who had ceased living long ago, but was too stubborn to go to hell.

He certainly looked barely alive. His pitifully lean frame beneath the battle-worn trail-coat had barely an ounce of spare flesh covering his skeleton. If any man deserved to be described as a living ghost, it was he.

Somehow he had managed to survive wounds and injuries that would have killed most normal men. His entire body was now little more than mutilated evidence of every single fight he had endured over the years.

His legend had grown as he stumbled from one bloody battle to another. Those who had encountered him and survived the experience knew that he was unlike any other man who rode through the Wild West. It was impossible to tell what his origins were. He had the height of a white man, yet did not look like one. His long, black hair was like that of an Indian, but no Indian ever looked like him. Whatever he was, he was rejected by everyone he ever met.

He did not belong in any world except the one of his own creation. It had a population of one.

Fuelled by cigar smoke, whiskey and jerky, he continued on through the trees, inhaling the scent of his prey as it grew stronger. His pair of matched Navy Colts in his deep coat-pockets hung like weights to either side of him as he spurred harder and harder. The blood-soaked mount beneath him obeyed fearfully. It knew its master was now ready for the kill.

Nothing could sway him now.

He was too close.

So close that he could smell the fear that dripped out of every pore on Kane's body as it hung on the night air. He jabbed his razor-sharp spurs into the flesh of his hard-pressed horse again and forced the tired animal to find even greater pace as it navigated between the pines.

The hunter of wanted men ignored the stress of the lathered-up mount beneath him as he had done with its countless predecessors. If it wanted food and water, it would have to find it for itself.

For the merciless bounty hunter would, without a second thought, ride until his mount collapsed and died. If necessary he would continue his relentless quest on foot, until his mission was completed.

Death rode on his shoulder.

It had always done so. The Grim Reaper had yet to claim his carcass and send him to the bowels of hell. Satan would have to be patient a little longer.

With the images and details of the wanted posters branded into his mind, the bounty hunter leaned back against his saddle cantle and drove his mount down through the trees with increased eagerness. His keen eyes had spotted the swaying grass on the edge of the vast rolling range. Kane's horse had driven a trail through it when the outlaw had at last managed to escape the tree-covered hills.

As the weary mount cleared the edge of the woodland, the bounty hunter dragged back on his reins, dismounted and stared out across the chest-high grass. Even the darkness of night could not prevent him from focusing on his chosen target. He could see the outlaw vainly attempting to get out of range of his pursuer's weaponry in the moon-light.

The tall emaciated figure pulled both his Navy Colts from his pockets and dragged their hammers back with his thumbs. He raised them, stared down through their sights and then squeezed the triggers. Deafening venom flashed from both barrels. The dapple grey bucked as it tossed the dead outlaw Daniel Kane from its saddle.

Satisfied at his handiwork, the bounty hunter dropped both smoking guns back into his coat pockets. He turned to his own horse and stepped toward the saddle. His bony fingers opened the satchel of his closer saddle-bag and pulled out a fresh bottle of whiskey. His small sharp teeth pulled the cork from its neck.

He spat it at the ground, raised the bottle to his thin lips and started to drink the fiery contents.

Iron Eyes would not lower the bottle of hard liquor until it was empty. The bounty hunter thought his job was finished. He was wrong.

It had only just started.

2

The fertile soil of the massive grassland range had drawn many people to the vast Arizona territory since the war had ended and the quest for peace had started. Most were simply looking for a place where they could raise crops and animals to give their families the chance of a future better than the past they had left behind them.

Yet some had been attracted to this place for far less honourable reasons. They had been lured by their insatiable appetites for greed and power. Like human leeches the corrupt minority had not taken long to gain control and suck the life-blood from their unwitting victims. Some call it civilization whilst others give it a far less worthy name. Corruption!

The numerous settlements which had sprung up across the newly opened-up territory did not take long to establish themselves. Temporary tent-cities soon became permanent wood-and-brick townships as businesses started to buy goods and sell the homesteaders everything they required.

As with all new towns, the unscrupulous had quickly latched on to the honest, law-abiding people and proceeded to fleece them. It was a pattern that had been followed since the first white man had set foot on the land that was to become known as America.

Like a subtle cancer, the pattern of greed had silently spread until it devoured everything.

The largest of the towns to have risen amid the swaying grassland valley was called, simply, Hope. It was a name that had inspired its original settlers and signified their faith in the future. Yet after a mere handful of years, the name had become ironic. For Hope was the one thing the honest people who lived on the large ranges and in the town itself, were stripped of.

The skilled criminals who had followed its original settlers and allowed them to do all the hard work, now ruled Hope and the rest of the towns. Like most of their breed, they were clever men. They allowed others to toil as they themselves found easier ways to make their fortunes. Gambling-halls, saloons and brothels culled every penny from the naïve and gullible. Taxes and threats gathered up what was left.

It was not a new story. It had trailed the pioneers since the first wagon had set forth and aimed its teams of horses, mules and ox towards the uncharted West. The corrupt always gained control and then punished the less well-educated or well-armed people until they became little more than servants.

The names might have never quite been the same, yet the men were indistinguishable in their ruthlessness.

Among them was Brewster Fontaine. He was one of the few. The few who used their intelligence to gain control of those who initially trusted the tall, handsome Easterner. By the time the people of Hope and those who lived in the grasslands realized what was happening, it was too late.

There is an old saying that appearances can be deceptive. It was true. Fontaine had the sophisticated demeanour of a riverboat gambler. His looks were those of a gentleman, yet in truth he was a heartless rogue. Unlike those he cheated, he had never actually worked with his hands for a living. He had never toiled in the sun and had his skin burned by its merciless rays. With a subtle hint of grey at the temples and a full head of neatly trimmed dark hair he had always been able to sway any females he encountered long enough for him to get the better of their menfolk.

With a cunning and ruthless soul, Fontaine had managed to enrich himself far beyond even his own imaginings. The territory had been good to him. He owned the only bank in Hope and almost every other business inside its boundaries. His interests stretched like the web of a spider to almost every other town along the wide range. He even held the mortgages on more than half the ranches and farms within a hundred square miles of Hope.

Yet Fontaine was troubled.

The looming prospect of statehood and interference from outside forces had made the businessman nervous. For the first time since he had arrived in the fertile Arizona territory, he was looking at the possibility of his power being reduced, if not completely destroyed. The laws which governed the rest of the Union might soon be enforced here.

Fontaine knew he had to do something, but what?

With an army of killers on his payroll he could control anyone within the borders of the territory's most prosperous region, but what would happen if Uncle Sam sent in the cavalry?

What if they placed a governor here?

The tall Fontaine knew that it would not take long for lawyers to drift in and unravel the empire he had spent a quarter of his life creating.

Men of Fontaine's sort never gave up without a fight though. They knew that there was always a way to get what you wanted if you desired it badly enough. Fate could be manipulated if you were capable of grasping the opportunity when it arose.

Then, as Fontaine stood on the veranda of his large home on the outskirts of Hope, he saw something riding towards him in the first rays of a new day. At first he thought it was just an Indian. Then he became uncertain as his eyes focused on the thin emaciated rider leading a horse through the tall grass. The sight of the dead body tied over the saddle made Fontaine aware that this was no Indian.

The businessman snapped his fingers.

'Riley!' Fontaine called out to his top

gun. 'Get out here fast!'

Frank Riley ran with his napkin still tucked like a bib into the top of his shirt. The gunslinger chewed and then swallowed the last of his breakfast as his thick, sturdy legs reached his employer.

'What ya want, boss?'

Fontaine raised a finger and aimed it at the rider who was approaching them slowly.

'What you figure that is, Riley?'

Riley shielded his eyes from the low, rising sun.

'Injun?'

'Whatever that is,' Fontaine drawled, 'I don't reckon it's an Indian, Riley!'

'He got himself a body tied over the saddle of that grey he's leading.' The gunman nodded.

'Ain't that Kane's grey?' Fontaine asked, clenching both his fists. 'It is!'

'Yep! It sure is! That's Kane's grey OK!' Riley gasped as he stroked the grips of his holstered .45s. 'Whoever that *hombre* is, he's found one of our best boys, boss!'

14

Brewster Fontaine shook his head and looked at his top gun.

'Found? I'm willing to wager he killed our young Daniel, Riley!'

'Who'd be capable of gettin' the better of Kane, boss?'

Fontaine gritted his teeth.

'Someone after the bounty on his head!'

'A bounty hunter?' Riley rubbed the sweat off his temples and screwed his eyes up even harder as they focused on the rider. 'Are ya sure it's a bounty hunter?'

'What other kind of man would have the nerve to come here with his kill, Riley?' Fontaine snarled.

'A bounty hunter?' The gunman repeated the description and then felt a shiver trace up his spine as sweat started to flow down it.

'Yeah, a bounty hunter!' Fontaine licked his lips. 'And I reckon that there's only one who could do that and come out of it unscathed, Riley!'

'Who?'

'Look at the critter!' Fontaine sighed. 'Long hair like an Indian. A bag of bones on horseback. There's only one man who fits that description and his name's Iron Eyes!'

Riley swallowed again.

'I thought he was dead!'

'Maybe he is!'

3

As with all creatures that prey upon others, Iron Eyes had spotted the two men standing upon the veranda of the large house on the outskirts of the sprawling town long before they had seen him. He had also studied what lay a few hundred yards behind the wooden sign with the word HOPE painted upon it. An array of wooden and brick buildings still slept as the two men watched his slow approach. They had watched him for more than five minutes. Two men of utterly different design. Although they were of equal height, that was where the similarity ended. One was dressed in leather and denim and had a seasoned gunbelt strapped around his stocky girth. Two holsters hung on either hip. It was obvious from the two leather laces tied around the man's thighs that this was a man who knew how to use his weaponry. He had gunslinger written all over his worthless hide.

Iron Eyes' icy glare also noted that the other man was undoubtedly wealthy. Very wealthy. Even from a half-mile away, the bounty hunter had been struck by how clean his clothes looked. Neat, tailored clothing that fitted perfectly. It was clear to Iron Eyes which one of the pair was the boss.

When the bounty hunter was less than a hundred feet from Fontaine's house, Iron Eyes' bony hands turned the reins at the last moment and aimed his horse towards the heart of the town.

He continued to watch the pair who studied him from the veranda until they were no longer in sight. Then his bullet-coloured eyes darted to what lay directly ahead.

Iron Eyes then concentrated on the rest of the town as he slowly headed into its main street. It looked peaceful enough, but he knew that it was never wise to take anything at face value. He bore the scars of that painful lesson.

Buildings of brick and wood stretched off as far as the eye could see in several directions. Yet the streets were empty. The rider knew that few townsfolk ever got up out of their warm beds before they had to.

Seeing the sheriff's office sign swaying from an overhang a few hundred feet ahead of him, Iron Eyes jabbed his spurs into the flesh of his lathered-horse and gave the body on the grey behind him a glance. The bounty on Daniel Kane was worth $1,000 dead or alive. The horse belied its own weariness and gathered pace in a vain attempt to outrun the bloodstained spurs.

The bounty hunter reined in and looped his long, thin right leg over the neck of his mount. Iron Eyes slid to the ground and secured his reins firmly to the closest hitching-rail. He ran his fingers through his own mane of long hair and pushed its matted strands away from his eyes.

He looked all around the street. Only when satisfied that there were no guns aimed in his direction did he untie the reins of the grey from his stirrup. Then he led the grey to the side of his own mount. He wrapped the reins around the wooden hitching-pole, then used an even tighter knot to ensure that the animal who carried his precious cargo did not wander away.

Iron Eyes stepped up on to the boardwalk and turned the doorknob of the sheriff's office. The door was locked up tight.

The deadly hunter of human vermin licked his dry lips and then moved to a wooden upright. He continued to study Hope. There were at least four side-streets from the main thoroughfare. As always, Iron Eyes was working out the safest route out of town should he be required to make a fast departure. There had been many times when the collective weaponry of a settlement had been turned on him.

He trusted no one!

Then the morning silence was broken. Iron Eyes heard the sound of a buggy's springs to his left. He tilted his head and stared through the limp strands of hair which hung before his gruesome features. Three well-armed horsemen trailed the buggy as it started down the main street towards him. Iron Eyes focused on the driver of the single-horse vehicle. It was the same man who had watched his approach from the veranda of the town's largest house, he thought.

'I wonder who them folks are?' Iron Eyes asked himself in a low whisper. He dropped his hands into the deep coat-pockets and pulled out his pair of Navy Colts. He tucked their long barrels into his belt. Their grips stuck out from his thin waist. 'If'n ya want trouble, keep a comin'!'

They did.

Fontaine led his small trio of riders down the middle of the main street towards the two exhausted horses tied up outside the sheriff's office and the

21

tall thin man who aimed his deadly stare at them.

The buggy slowed as Fontaine eased back on the reins, then pushed the brake-pole forward with his highly polished right shoe. The three horsemen encircled their employer and aimed their horses' noses at the bounty hunter.

There was no hint of emotion on Iron Eyes' hideous face.

'I see that you've been busy, stranger!' Fontaine said as he stepped down from the buggy and dusted his clothing off with gloved hands.

'Yep!' Iron Eyes snarled through gritted teeth. 'It got anythin' to do with you?'

Fontaine smiled and removed his hat. He held it across his midriff and stepped a little closer to the man who continued to rest a shoulder against the upright.

'I'd like it if you showed me a little respect. I happen to own this town and most of the range, mister! If I wanted to, I'd have you shot for trespassing. Do you understand?'

There was still no emotion on the carved features of the bounty hunter. He continued to stare at Fontaine and the three gunmen astride their horses behind him.

'You could try, dude!' Iron Eyes sighed. 'I'd not recommend it, though! You might die!'

The gunmen eased their mounts forward. They stopped when their employer raised a hand.

'Easy, boys! We got us a spirited man here! We don't want to spook him, do we?'

'Let me and the boys see to him, boss!' Riley requested angrily. 'We'll teach him a lesson he'll not forget!'

Iron Eyes straightened up. He narrowed his eyes.

'Try it, fat boy!' he growled at the horseman. 'It'd be a pleasure killin' you!'

Fontaine waved his hand again. 'Easy! We don't want to wake up the folks around here this early! I'm sure Iron Eyes is just a tad tired!'

The bounty hunter's eyes darted at the well-dressed man below him in the street. He tilted his head and stared through his limp strands of hair.

'You know my name?'

Fontaine smiled again. This time it looked even less friendly.

'It was just a lucky guess! Your reputation precedes you!'

Iron Eyes raised his left hand slowly and plucked a cigar from his shirt-pocket. He bit off its tip, spat it out, then gripped the long length between his teeth.

'Then ya know I'm a bounty hunter?' he asked, producing a match from the same pocket and running his thumbnail across it. He raised the flame to the cigar and sucked in the smoke. 'Ya know that all I want is my bounty money!'

Fontaine toyed with his hat.

'This is awkward for me, Iron Eyes!'

'How come?' Iron Eyes asked from a cloud of smoke.

'I own the bank that is meant to pay bounties, but I also used to employ young Daniel here!'

'So?'

'It grieves me to pay out money for having one of my boys gunned down, Iron Eyes!' Fontaine shrugged. 'It sets a bad example, if you get my drift?'

Riley edged his horse closer to the grey and pointed at the body tied over its saddle. Flies had gathered on the dried bloodstains on the back of his fellow outlaw.

'Look! Kane was backshot! Ya shot him in the back, Iron Eyes!'

Iron Eyes sucked in more smoke.

'Sure I did! He was ridin' away from me! If'n he'd bin braver, I'd have shot him in the front!'

Fontaine bit his lip. He knew that anyone who looked the way Iron Eyes looked might be capable of killing them all if he was forced. It did not pay to square up to anyone of his kind.

'I reckon I can make an exception in your case, Iron Eyes!' he started. 'I'll pay the bounty and claim it back from the authorities down in Texas!'

Iron Eyes nodded.

'That's smart!' he declared.

Fontaine stepped back up into his buggy and gathered the reins together. He stared at the grim bounty hunter.

'My name's Brewster Fontaine, Iron Eyes! It's a name that you ought to be wary of!'

'The only names that interest me are the ones on Wanted posters, Fontaine!' Iron Eyes said bluntly. 'You on any Wanted posters?'

'Don't push your luck!' Fontaine snarled.

The bounty hunter looked at the three mounted gunmen. He inhaled deeply, then glanced back at their employer.

'I can't recall ever seein' you on any posters, Fontaine, but I sure recognize them boys of yours! Must be at least two thousand dollars sitting on them horses! Temptin'! Yep, mighty temptin'!'

'They ain't all my boys, Iron Eyes!'

the businessman declared loudly. 'I got a whole army of guns, if you're interested? So don't mess with me! OK? Even you couldn't take on all of my boys!'

Iron Eyes chewed on the cigar.

'OK! Just don't forget to have that bounty money ready at the bank when I come callin'!'

'You better spend it fast, Iron Eyes.' Fontaine smiled. 'I have a feeling that you ain't going to live long!'

The most powerful man in Hope released the brake and lashed his reins across the back of the horse harnessed in the traces before him. The buggy sped off with the three outriders eating its dust.

Iron Eyes tapped the ash from his cigar and then spotted a white-haired man coming towards him from the opposite direction. The man had a gleaming star pinned to his black vest.

'You responsible for killin' that crit-ter, boy?' the sheriff asked. He pulled the office key from his vest-pocket and pushed it into the lock.

'Yep!' Iron Eyes replied, staring down at the man.

'That's one of Fontaine's boys.' The sheriff opened the door and wandered slowly inside. 'No wonder he was lookin' a mite ornery!'

The bounty hunter trailed the lawman into the office interior as the man raised the blinds and allowed the morning sun to flood in.

'You belong to that Fontaine critter too, Sheriff?' Iron Eyes asked.

The sheriff looked at the tall man and shrugged sheepishly.

'In a way, son! In a way!'

Iron Eyes rested a hip on the desk.

'Is it true that he's got himself an army of hired guns?'

The sheriff nodded fearfully.

'If eighty or ninety gunslingers make an army, then he's got one! Why?'

Iron Eyes sucked on the cigar and tightened his eyes.

'I never had me a fight with a whole army before!' He sighed.

4

In common with all saloons in towns on the edge of civilization, the Spinning Wheel rarely closed its doors for long. Just for enough time to brush out the old sawdust and replace it with fresh. Enough time for cigar smoke to filter its way out of the numerous bullet holes in its weathered wooden walls.

The Spinning Wheel was a two-storey structure half-way down Hope's main street and directly opposite the solid brick bank building. It suited the bounty hunter perfectly. He was dry and required a place to wait until the bank opened up its doors for business.

He had left the aged sheriff to dispose of Kane's body and led his tired mount to the place which stank of a mixture of human sweat and stale liquor. Yet its aroma meant nothing to the tall bounty hunter. His flared nostrils still had the acrid stench of death in them. Kane's body had started to rot fast when the morning sun had risen over the range. It had taken hours to reach this town with the lifeless carcass. The smell of sweat was a welcome change.

Iron Eyes strolled in through the swing-doors and watched as the bartender scattered fresh sawdust from a pail on to the freshly mopped floor.

'Ya open for business?'

'Yep. I'm open for business!' The bartender nodded and returned behind the long mahogany counter which was stacked with thimble glasses. 'What'll it be?'

Iron Eyes strode up to the bar, rested a boot on its brass rail and pointed at the bottles on a shelf in front of a rectangular mirror.

'A bottle of ya best rye!'

The bartender lifted one of the bottles off the shelf and placed it before the bounty hunter. Iron Eyes' thin hands placed a gleaming ten-dollar gold piece down on to the wet surface.

'Don't see many gold pieces in these parts,' the bartender noted as he scooped it up and moved to his cash register. 'First one I seen in over a year.'

'I always insist on being paid in coin!' Iron Eyes said. He pulled the cork from the bottle-neck and sniffed at the whiskey. 'I don't like paper money!'

'What line of work ya in?' the man asked, gathering up the change to return to his only customer before dropping the gold coin into the register's tray.

Iron Eyes took one of the small thimble glasses from the stack and looked at it.

'I'm a hunter!' he replied before replacing the glass and lifting the bottle to his lips.

'What kinda hunter?' the bartender asked innocently as he watched Iron Eyes take a long swallow from the bottle. 'Ain't much game in these parts.

31

What's ya speciality?'

Iron Eyes lowered the bottle and sighed.

'Men! I hunt men!' he answered.

'Men?'

'Bad men!' Iron Eyes added.

The bartender felt his legs start to shake. He had served thousands of customers in his time, but none quite like this strange man.

'You serious?' he croaked nervously.

Iron Eyes nodded slowly and went to return the bottle to his lips when he saw movement in the street through one of the saloon's windows. He rested the whiskey on the counter and stared at the growing crowd of well-armed men which was gathering between the saloon and the bank.

'I'm a bounty hunter, barkeep!' he explained. He pointed one of his bony fingers at the crowd. 'They work for Fontaine?'

'How'd ya know that?'

'Lucky guess!' Iron Eyes stretched his long legs and strode to the nearest window. He stared at the men. Each of them was a hired gun. Every one of them wore a fancy shooting rig. Only gunslingers and outlaws could afford that sort of armoury, he thought.

'They lookin' for you?' the bartender asked fearfully.

'I'd not bet against it!' Iron Eyes said. He turned and walked back to the bar, the man and his bottle. 'Don't get scared. They ain't ready to start nothin' yet!'

'How can ya tell?'

Iron Eyes lifted the bottle, took another swift swig from its neck, then returned it to the wet circle on the wooden counter.

'There ain't enough of them yet.'

'What ya mean? I can count twenty or more from here.'

'That ain't enough!' Iron Eyes said. 'Fontaine wants to try and impress me before he sets his pack of dogs on me. They reckon he's got around eighty or ninety gunmen on his payroll, don't they?'

'At least that many!' The bartender nodded.

'Then we got us a whole lot more comin', barkeep!' Iron Eyes dragged both his Navy Colts from his deep coat-pockets and pushed their blue steel barrels into his belt. 'That kinda critter don't dare fight alone. They like to be part of a crowd.'

'You tryin' to say that them boys out there in the street are cowards?'

Iron Eyes pulled out a half-smoked cigar and rammed it between his teeth. The bartender struck a match and leant across the counter. The bounty hunter accepted the flame and sucked it into the cigar.

'I ain't sure what they are just yet!' he said. 'But they don't seem too eager to cross the street and come on in here, do they?'

'What does Fontaine have against ya, mister?' There was genuine concern in the bartender's voice. 'What ya done to upset him?'

Iron Eyes inhaled on the cigar and

stared through the smoke at the far smaller man.

'I killed one of his boys and he owes me a lotta reward money!'

'That ain't good! A lotta folks around here have died for a lot less than that!'

Iron Eyes gave a crooked smile.

'But it is interestin' though, ain't it? Makes ya wonder what that Fontaine varmint intends doin' to me! He's just dumb enough to try and get them boys to kill me.'

'How come ya ain't scared, mister?' the bartender asked, curious. 'Who the hell are ya? How come ya ain't scared?'

'They call me Iron Eyes!'

There was a shocked expression on the man's face. 'I've heard a lotta stories about you. They say that you're the most deadly bounty hunter there is! They also say that ya can't be killed!'

'What's your name?'

'Ted. Ted Cooper,' the bartender stuttered.

'Some stories about me are a tad tall, Ted.' Iron Eyes returned his gaze to the windows. The crowd was getting larger with every passing moment.

'Which of them are true?'

'Ya might find out darn soon, Ted,' Iron Eyes said wryly. He then heard the sound of hoofs echoing from the street. Iron Eyes straightened up and bit his lower lip as his eyes focused on the rider with the morning sun on his back. Through the open saloon doors he could see Frank Riley whipping his mount towards the rest of the men.

'That's Frank Riley! He's Fontaine's top gun!' Cooper observed.

'I know who he is! I also know that he's worth over a thousand bucks dead or alive!' Iron Eyes muttered. He looked around the large room. 'Where's the stairs up to the second floor, Ted?'

The bartender raised his eyebrows. He then pointed at a door in the corner of the room.

'There! But what ya wanna go up there for, Iron Eyes?'

'Would ya believe that I got me a real

cravin' to take in the scenery?' Iron Eyes replied.

'Nope.' Cooper shrugged.

'You ain't as dumb as ya look, Ted!' Iron Eyes pulled his guns from his belt and cocked their hammers. 'Keep ya head down until the shootin' stops!'

The bartender watched as the tall figure walked slowly towards the door. Iron Eyes gripped the handle and paused.

'Guard my bottle, Ted Cooper! Guard it with ya life! I'll be back!'

The bartender nodded silently as the bounty hunter disappeared into the shadows. He could hear the blood-stained spurs jangle as Iron Eyes ascended to the second floor.

5

Like moths being drawn to a naked flame, more of Fontaine's henchmen gathered in the main street as Frank Riley rallied his troops. The gunslinger had received his orders from Brewster Fontaine and was executing them to the letter. Fifty-eight of the most ruthless men on Fontaine's payroll were in town and every one of them had been gathered up and ordered to stand between the bank and the strange bounty hunter. If Iron Eyes wanted his blood-money, he would have to face each and every one of them to get it. Most ordinary men might have taken the hint and decided that it was just not worth the trouble.

But not Iron Eyes. He was not so easily frightened.

Riley remained mounted as the well-paid hired guns stood across the front of the bank building. Some had walked there whilst others had ridden from the furthest corners of the sprawling town of Hope. But they had all come as commanded for fear of disobeying their paymaster.

'Remember, boys,' Riley shouted. 'I don't wanna see Iron Eyes gettin' into the bank! Them's my orders! He don't get in there and he don't get no bounty! Savvy?'

There were noises that drifted in unison from all the gunslingers' lips as they nodded at Riley.

'Good!' The top gun laughed. 'Now get ya guns out of them holsters and cock them hammers!'

Again, as one, the gunslingers all drew their guns and pulled back their hammers.

'Can we kill him?' a voice called out from somewhere in the middle of the crowd.

'We might have to kill the bastard!' Riley laughed. 'He might be one of them loco folks that don't take tellin'!'

Every one of the gunslingers gave out a loud cheer that filled the street. These were men who had tasted the thrill of killing many times and savoured its unwholesome flavour.

Riley swung his mount around and grinned at the bounty hunter's pitiful horse tied up outside the Spinning Wheel. He knew that even if Iron Eyes did manage to escape their guns, he would not get far on that animal.

It had been ridden to exhaustion.

'We got the back-shootin' bastard cornered, boys!' Riley chuckled out loud as he steadied his horse. 'I don't figure he'll try to cross the street to get his money! I got me a feelin' Iron Eyes will run when he sets eyes on us!'

Suddenly a noise drew their attention to the balcony of the saloon. It was the sound of a window being opened up on the second floor. The hired guns watched silently as Iron Eyes stepped out on to its weathered balcony.

It was an awesome sight, which chilled even the most hardened of them. A unified gasp went through the hired gunmen.

Iron Eyes had both his Navy Colts gripped in his bony hands as he strode across to the wooden rails and gazed angrily down on them.

'Look, Frank!' one of the gunslingers shouted. 'What in tarnation is that?'

'That's the critter we gotta stop gettin' into the bank, ya dumb bastard!' Riley felt his heart start pounding inside his chest. Few men could set eyes upon the gaunt bounty hunter's scarred features without feeling totally horrified.

Iron Eyes moved behind the large wooden façade which had the name 'Spinning Wheel Saloon' painted upon it. He stood like a macabre statue watching the large group of men, his guns aimed down at them.

'Ya lookin' for me, ya fat fool?' Iron Eyes asked from his lofty perch. 'Ya still thinkin' of tryin' ya luck?'

Riley felt his mouth and throat drying.

'Ya don't scare me, ya freak! I've killed worse-lookin' folks than you in my time!'

'There ain't nobody worse-lookin' than me, ya liar!' the bounty hunter drawled.

'Ya better ride on out of Hope, Iron Eyes!' Riley waved a hand at the man who looked down on them. 'Ride out or we'll kill ya for sure!'

'Ya got a lot of guts when enough of ya gather together!' the gaunt figure shouted down at Fontaine's men. 'It don't bother me none though! I'll kill ya all if'n that's what it takes for me to get paid!'

Riley steadied his mount again. Unlike its master, it had horse sense and wanted to flee.

'We bin ordered to make sure ya don't get one red cent, Iron Eyes!' Riley shouted. 'It'd be best if ya just rode out of this town and kept on going until this territory is just a bad memory!'

'Ya deaf or somethin', Riley?' Iron Eyes questioned. 'I just told ya that I'll kill ya all to get what I'm owed! That ain't no threat, that's what they call a prophecy!'

'How ya gonna manage that, Iron Eyes?' Riley laughed. 'Ya only got twelve bullets in them guns! Can't ya count? There gotta be sixty or more of us here! Fontaine got even more men around the range! Well?'

'I count fifty-nine,' the bounty hunter contradicted. 'Don't go frettin' about how many bullets I got, Riley! My coat pockets are full of ammunition. I could put two shells in each of ya and still have a few left over for ya boss!'

Riley looked at the men behind him. The smiles had long gone from their troubled faces. They were starting to get nervous of the sheer arrogance of the bounty hunter. He gritted his teeth and yelled out loud.

'We gonna let that scarecrow bad mouth us, boys? He ain't nothin' but a back-shooter! His breed don't have a chance against real gunmen!'

The men gave a reasoned grunt.

None of them was willing to let the rest see his fear. Riley turned back, gathered up his reins and smiled at the man who held both his Navy Colts at hip-level, with their barrels trained down at them.

'Ya gonna die, bounty hunter!' Riley laughed. 'It'll be slow and darn painful! Well?'

Iron Eyes did not move an inch.

'I'm tryin' to keep my temper, Riley! The law would be on my side if I killed you all just like I did Kane! Outlaws wanted dead or alive don't deserve no favours from me!'

'There ain't no law in these parts!' Riley snarled loudly. 'Only gun law!'

Iron Eyes stroked the hammers of his guns with his thumbs.

'That's my favourite sort!'

Swiftly, Riley dismounted and led his horse through the gunslingers. As he reached the narrow alley at the side of the bank he shouted out:

'Kill him, boys! Kill him! He wants to eat lead, so fill his worthless belly!'

Every finger squeezed a trigger. No thunderclap could have sounded louder as lethal lead exploded from the barrels of the gunslingers' guns.

A dense choking cloud of gunsmoke filled the street and shielded all view of the tall, defiant bounty hunter. Iron Eyes had felt the heat of the first few bullets as they passed within inches of his lean frame. His long loose coat tails were lifted up as hot lead tore through the seasoned fabric.

He quickly stepped backwards.

Yet Iron Eyes did not return fire.

He knew Riley had been correct when he had said that his trusty guns only held twelve bullets between them. Iron Eyes knew that he had to ensure that he did not waste any of his precious ammunition. It took time to reload, and that time might be the difference between life and death.

The thin-framed man stooped and ran unseen to the end of the long balcony. He knelt, screwed up his eyes and aimed at the men who continued to fire their deafening volleys of bullets up at the saloon's façade.

Then he started.

One by one he picked off the gunslingers. Each one of his bullets found its target. Gunmen spun on their boot-heels before crashing into the sand. Within seconds the ground was stained crimson.

It reminded the bounty hunter of days when he had witnessed the wholesale slaughter of the buffalo herds on the plains. The hunters would simply move downwind toward the grazing herds and then start to pick off the animals one by one. For some reason that Iron Eyes had never been able to fathom, the buffalo would see animals fall after being shot, but they remained grazing.

Just like the buffalo, the hired gunmen did not seem to grasp what was happening to them. With bodies falling, they continued to fire up to where they had last seen the bounty hunter. Not one of them realized that their chosen prey was no longer behind the saloon's façade. They seemed incapable of understanding that Iron Eyes was picking them off from the corner of the balcony.

Perhaps it was because the street was filled with black acrid gunsmoke, which blinded the gunslingers' view of their target. Maybe it was because their own weaponry was making such a deafening din that they could not hear that the shots were coming from a different direction.

Whatever the reason, Iron Eyes was not about to turn down a gift horse. He would continue picking off Fontaine's small army with deadly accuracy. Yet with every squeeze of his triggers he kept seeing the images of the buffalo in his mind's eye.

Unlike the rest of the gunmen gathered in the street, Riley had yet to use his own guns. He remained in the alley beside the bank and watched like a seasoned army general.

This was not the way it was meant to

be. Riley glanced at the dozen or more bodies and tried to work out how one man could kill so many.

What he was witnessing confused him. With every beat of his black heart he was seeing one of his men drop lifelessly to the ground. He then realized that the shots that were felling his men were not coming from the façade. They were coming from the corner.

Riley ran to the opposite wall and frantically searched the balcony for Iron Eyes. It did not take long to spot the kneeling figure as he fired one gun after another.

Fontaine's top gun dragged one of his .45s from its holster and cocked the hammer. He shouted a warning at his men, but none of them could hear anything above the sound of their blazing guns. Riley looked again at the bounty hunter with the smoking guns in his hands. Again Iron Eyes fired. Another of the gunslingers fell face first into the sand.

'I'm gonna pluck ya like a Thanks-giving turkey, Iron Eyes!' Riley spat. He raised his gun and aimed at the painfully thin target.

The gunslinger's .45 unleashed its lead in a plume of smoke and red-hot flame. Riley fired again. He had not lived to his forty-second year for nothing. He was a good shot.

Riley dragged his other Colt and fired both weapons. He smiled in satisfaction as the wooden rails that Iron Eyes was kneeling behind shat-tered and blasted splinters into the bounty hunter's face.

Iron Eyes screwed up his eyes. No porcupine's quills could have inflicted more blinding pain.

Riley's next two shots came even closer to the determined bounty hunter. More hot slivers of wooden fragments hit Iron Eyes straight in the face when the hot lead smashed two more rails into mere matchsticks.

Iron Eyes fell backwards in agony and landed on his bony spine. The skin around his eyes was bleeding from the countless splinters embedded in his flesh.

He rolled over until he was on his knees. He dropped his weapons on to the boards of the balcony and feverishly tore the sharp wooden fragments from his face. Blood flowed like water over Iron Eyes' hands and fingers as he tried to pull the slivers of wood from his flesh.

'Now I'm damn angry, fat man!' Iron Eyes snatched up his Navy Colts and rubbed the blood from his face across the back of his sleeve. He was looking through a swirling fog, trying desperately to see the gunman. At last his vision cleared enough for him to see Riley blasting both his guns at him from the side of the bank. Vainly Iron Eyes returned fire until the chambers of his trusty guns were empty.

Again Riley's bullets forced the bounty hunter even further back from the edge of the balcony. Iron Eyes snarled as his fingers searched in his deep pockets for bullets to reload his guns. He scooped out a handful, dropped them on to the boards and shook the spent casings from the smoking weapons.

The blood on his fingers made the bullets slippery as he tried to push them into the smoking chambers. It felt like an eternity before he managed to achieve this simple goal. For the first time since the gunfight had started, the bounty hunter realized that he was cornered.

Iron Eyes snapped both chambers shut and pulled the hammers back with his thumbs.

Frank Riley ran to his men and pointed to where he knew the bounty hunter was trapped. Within a few seconds every one of the hired guns was firing up at the balcony.

Burning sawdust fell like a blizzard's snow over the crouching figure as Iron Eyes' mind raced. There had to be a way out of this fix, he told himself. If there was, Iron Eyes had yet to figure it.

All he could do was try and avoid the lethal volley of bullets that kept him pinned down. He looked through the wooden railings to where he had left his exhausted horse. The animal was still there but it was dead. Countless shots had torn chunks out of the horse's flesh.

'Keep shootin'! We got the critter stuck, boys!' Riley shouted at the thirty or so remaining hired guns. 'He can't go no place from there!'

Another of the gunslingers who went by the name of Keno moved to Riley's side and tugged at the man's sleeve.

'How we gonna get him down from there?'

'I got me an idea, Keno!' Riley said. He ran to his horse and dragged the rope from its saddle horn. Riley swiftly looped it over the horn and tightened it, then led his horse through his men to one of the balcony's four supports. He wrapped the rope around the wooden pole several times, then tied a secure knot.

'What ya doin' that for, Frank?' another of the gunslingers asked as he watched the top gun mount the nervous animal.

'If'n Iron Eyes won't come down,' Riley answered, 'I figured we ought to bring him down!'

As his men fired over the dead bodies of their fellow hired guns, Riley spurred hard and forced his mount to haul at the wooden support. The rope went taut and started to vibrate. Riley spurred and spurred. The wooden pole began to crack under the strain. Then it gave and was dragged away from the boardwalk. The gunman dismounted and untied the rope. Riley threw it to Keno who then looped it around the end upright, directly beneath the corner of the balcony. Riley leapt back on to his saddle and drove his spurs into his animal's flanks.

The rope tightened once more as the horse pulled.

Iron Eyes realized what was happening and got to his feet. He started to run back towards the façade when he felt the boards beneath his boots move. The bounty hunter stopped and saw a gap appear between the saloon wall and the balcony. The entire length creaked and swayed.

Iron Eyes was still thirty feet from the open window that he had used to step out on to the balcony, but there were a few closed ones next to him.

The sound of lumber breaking under the strain of being pulled away from the wall was so loud that, for a brief moment, Iron Eyes had not been able to hear the guns below him. Nails flew like daggers in all directions. Iron Eyes tried to steady himself as the boards beneath his boots began to fall away. He could see the boardwalk through the gaps as planks fell to the ground.

There was no time to waste. Iron Eyes had to act and act fast.

As Riley's horse eventually managed to drag the corner upright away, the bounty hunter leapt for the nearest window.

The guns in his outstretched hands shattered the panes as his thin body followed them through the window frame. Iron Eyes landed heavily in a bedroom amid a million slivers of glass. He steadied himself and then spotted a six-inch piece of broken glass sticking out of his leg. He pulled it out and tossed it aside.

With blood pouring from the jagged gash, he staggered to his feet and glanced out of the window just as the entire balcony disintegrated and collapsed. A cloud of dust billowed up from the street.

'This is gettin' darn painful!' Iron Eyes snarled under his breath. He limped across the room, opened the door and then ignoring his own pain, rushed into the corridor.

The sound of gunfire was no quieter even in the centre of the building. Yet Iron Eyes ignored it and forged on. Somehow the bleeding figure moved like quicksilver along the carpeted corridor until he found the staircase which led down into the heart of the saloon.

He had left a trail of blood in his wake.

Iron Eyes walked down the dark stairwell and paused behind the door. He could still hear the shooting echoing inside the Spinning Wheel from the street. He pushed the door open with the barrels of his guns and narrowed his eyes.

The bartender was still hiding behind the mahogany bar counter. Except for him, the huge room was empty. Riley and his men were still firing their guns at shadows in the smoke and dust.

Iron Eyes walked from the door and behind the bar. He stopped above the shaking bartender.

'Give me my bottle, Ted Cooper!' Iron Eyes demanded.

Cooper did as commanded and gave the bottle of rye to the bleeding figure. He watched in stunned awe as the bounty hunter raised the whiskey above his head and poured its fiery contents over his face and then the wound in his leg.

'That's gotta hurt!' Cooper exclaimed.

Iron Eyes nodded, then took a long swallow from the bottle's neck. He exhaled heavily and placed the bottle down on the counter.

'Got any cigars?'

The bartender raised both eyebrows and picked a box off the shelves next to him. He opened its lid and picked one out for the injured man beside him.

Iron Eyes accepted the cigar and bit off its tip. He placed it between his teeth and straightened up. His eyes were still not seeing clearly. He heard the match being struck and allowed the bartender to light his cigar for him.

'Thanks, *amigo*!' the bounty hunter said through a cloud of smoke.

'What ya gonna do?' Cooper asked.

'Reckon I'm either gonna die or I might get lucky!'

Cooper stood up beside the taller man. He stared at the gruesome face, which had blood trailing from untold cuts around the eyes.

'There's too many of them!' the bartender said firmly.

'There usually are!' Iron Eyes sighed as he sucked more smoke into his lungs. 'They killed my horse! I've gotta stay here now and try and finish the rest of them critters off!'

'I got me a horse out back, Iron Eyes!' Cooper said. 'You can have it if'n ya wants! Well?'

'I ain't the sort to hightail it!' The bounty hunter's bleeding eyes stared through the windows at the wreckage of the balcony, which was piled up high outside the front of the virtually empty saloon. He knew that he still had some time left before any of his attackers would be able to get inside the Spinning Wheel, but he had to make a decision soon. Time was running out quickly.

'Ya ain't gotta chance against all of them boys!' Cooper insisted. 'They're scum!'

Iron Eyes took another long swallow

of the whiskey and then drew in smoke from the cigar. He flashed his eyes at the man beside him. A man who was showing concern.

'Fontaine owes me a thousand bucks, Ted! I ain't gonna ride out of this town without it!'

'I've got a small shack on the outskirts of town,' Cooper said. 'You can hole up there until dark. There's iodine and bandages there. You could fix up that leg. I finish work at seven tonight. I'll come and let ya know what's happening! What ya reckon?'

'I ain't sure why ya want to help me,' Iron Eyes muttered in a low tone. 'Most folks won't come within spittin' distance of me. How come ya want to help me?'

'Maybe I'm just sick of Fontaine and his vermin.' Cooper shrugged. 'Ya might be an ugly critter but ya a damn sight more honest than them killers out there! Maybe you can bring some justice to Hope!'

Iron Eyes nodded and grabbed a

handful of the cigars.

'OK! What kinda horse ya got out back?'

'He ain't much to look at, Iron Eyes. Just an old chestnut with grey whiskers on his chin, but he can still gallop.'

Iron Eyes slid the bottle into one of his deep pockets.

'OK!'

Cooper led the bleeding man out of the rear of the large building to the horse. He pointed to where his shack was situated at the town's edge and told him to let the old horse take him there. It knew the route by heart.

Iron Eyes slapped the reins across the shoulders of the animal and hung on tight. Cooper had been correct. The chestnut could still gallop. It also knew the shortest way through the back lanes to the bartender's small shack.

6

The sight which greeted Brewster
Fontaine was not what he had either
expected or could have imagined
possible. This was carnage. He pulled
back on his reins and stopped the
buggy a few dozen yards away from
the pile of blood-soaked bodies which
blocked the main street. The sun had
already started to do its worst and the
stench of death filled the main street.

Fontaine could not disguise his
horror as he stepped down on to the
ground and tried to understand what
had occurred. He had given orders for
his men to stop the bounty hunter from
entering the bank and getting his
reward money. There should have been
only one body lying on the sand. It
should have been Iron Eyes' carcass
attracting flies in the hot mid-morning
sun, not so many of his hired guns.

The pale face of the bank-manager stared out from in front of the solid building where Fontaine kept all his money. The man looked in shock and seemed unable to know what to do. He was shaking as he walked towards Fontaine.

'Sh . . . should I open up the bank, sir?' the banker asked.

'That's what I pay you to do, Sloane,' Fontaine said. His hands waved the terrified employee away. 'Open up and do your job!'

The man scurried away.

Again Fontaine looked at his rotting hired guns. So many men that it chilled him. He bit his lower lip and tried to hide his revulsion as he watched Frank Riley, Keno and a few of his surviving men approaching him.

He turned and looked at the twisted pile of wood which cluttered the front of the saloon.

'Did ya get Iron Eyes, Riley?' Fontaine asked as the men reached the buggy. 'Tell me that he's lying over there with them bodies!'

'He got away!' Riley managed to say. 'That critter just ain't human like us, boss! We had him cornered and he just up and vanished!'

'What?' Fontaine gasped. 'Do you say that Iron Eyes got away? He escaped? How?'

'Yep, boss.' Riley nodded. 'He just disappeared.'

'Like a damned ghost!' Keno added. 'They say that he ain't no living man, don't they? I reckon it's true. He's a ghost!'

Fontaine rolled his eyes and started to walk slowly towards the saloon.

'Ghosts don't kill folks, Keno! Iron Eyes might be many things but he ain't no ghost!'

'But he vanished, boss.' Riley pushed his hat back off his furrowed brow as he trailed the tall, handsome Fontaine. 'We searched everywhere for him and didn't find no trace of the varmint.'

The businessman sighed loudly and pointed at the bodies.

'How many of our men did he kill?'

'Twenty-three,' Riley replied quietly.

Fontaine shook his head. 'Twenty-three? That bag of bones killed twenty-three of the best guns in the territory?'

'We killed his horse!' Keno pointed at the body of Iron Eyes' mount.

'Damn shame that Iron Eyes wasn't sitting on the animal when you shot the worthless nag, ain't it?' Fontaine screamed. 'You might have accidentally managed to shoot him as well!'

The gunslingers walking beside the businessman went silent as they drew closer to the Spinning Wheel. They trailed Fontaine as he walked up to the front of the saloon and paused before the wreckage of the balcony strewn the length of the building.

The town was now awake and the street was filled with curious onlookers. This was the first time that any of the honest hard-working residents of Hope had seen Fontaine's grip on power challenged.

'Get them nosy bastards off the boardwalks, Riley!' Fontaine ordered his men. 'I don't want to have them gloating at my expense.'

Riley ushered his remaining men towards the crowd of interested towns-folk and started to force them off the streets and into the buildings, where their muted laughter might not reach Fontaine's ears.

Fontaine stepped cautiously up on to the loose planks of wood piled up outside the Spinning Wheels entrance and studied them carefully. Then he saw something which drew his attention. He bent down and touched one of the planks. A smiled etched his face.

'What ya found there, boss?' Keno asked as he rested a boot on the edge of the boardwalk.

Fontaine straightened up and showed the tips of his fingers to the gunman.

'Look at it, Keno! Look at it! What do you see?'

'Blood?' Keno answered.

'Exactly!' Fontaine smiled. 'Blood!

Ghosts don't bleed, do they? One of you useless bastards managed to hit his target!'

The rest of the gunmen gathered around their boss and stared at his crimson fingertips.

'This is the blood of Iron Eyes!' Fontaine announced. 'The blood of Iron Eyes!'

7

Blood covered the earthen floor where the wounded Iron Eyes had spent the previous hour. The bartender's humble shack was less than twelve feet square and had more holes in its roof than there were in the tails of Iron Eyes' coat. It had a small stove set in the corner with a stack which went up through the roof. The bounty hunter had spent every second he had been inside the shack feeding the stove with kindling until its blackened belly was red-hot. The stove's heat was unwelcome during the hottest part of the day but Iron Eyes knew it was necessary. The wounded man had lost too much blood and he had to stop the bleeding leg-wound quickly.

Iron Eyes stared at the fire and the poker which was buried in its flames.

The metal rod glowed like a branding-iron.

It was ready.

He had already dosed a whole bottle of iodine on to the deep bloody gash in his thigh through the hole he had ripped in his pants' leg. It had stung like a million hornet stings, but Iron Eyes knew there was a far worse pain to come. One that he had experienced many times before during his violent lifetime.

Iron Eyes removed his twisted cigar butt from his teeth and threw it into the flames. He then replaced it with one of his bullets. He gripped the brass casing firmly with his sharp teeth and then wrapped sacking around his right hand to protect it from the heat of the smoking poker.

Iron Eyes cautiously gripped the end of the poker and then withdrew its length from the stove's open door.

The tip of the poker was glowing red-hot.

Without a second's hesitation Iron

Eyes pressed it against the bleeding gash in his leg. It hissed like a viper. Smoke rose up into the air. The smell of burning flesh filled his flared nostrils. He bit down on the bullet with all his might and reeled away from the stove.

Pain ripped through his entire body.

The bounty hunter dropped the poker and staggered to the bed set against the opposite wall. His lean body fell on to its sheets.

Iron Eyes inhaled through his nostrils and rocked back and forth until he no longer felt the urge to scream out. He was still aware that the shack's walls were too thick for him to draw the attention of anyone that might be hunting him.

His heart pounded inside his chest like an Apache war drum as he fought the agonizing torture that he had inflicted upon himself.

He spat the bullet at the dirt floor.

Iron Eyes had lost a lot of blood yet somehow he had managed to retain consciousness. He forced himself to rise until he was upright and sitting with his long legs draped over the edge of the bed. He stared at his smouldering flesh visible through the torn hole in his pants' leg.

His skin had been crudely melted.

But the bleeding had stopped.

The weary bounty hunter gazed at the small solitary window covered in shredded sackcloth. Sunlight filtered through it into the shack. The day was still young but he was once again unable to do anything except wait for his strength to return. He knew that he was in trouble.

Big trouble.

Iron Eyes dragged the bottle of whiskey off the floor and lifted its neck to his lips. He did not lower it until he had consumed its entire contents. Then he dropped it on to the earth at his feet.

His fingers found one of the cigars that Ted Cooper had given him. He placed it between his teeth. He chewed on its end and tried to control his breathing as his heart began to slow down to somewhere close to normal.

The cuts on his face had already scabbed and the dried blood felt like a mask covering his flesh. Sweat dripped from the limp strands of hair which hung before his unblinking eyes.

He rested his back against the wooden wall and stared at the still-smoking poker resting on the dirt floor where he had dropped it. He pulled both his guns from his coat pockets, cocked their hammers and set them to either side of him a few inches from his hands. It was a ritual he had practised countless times before in divers places.

His Navy Colts were always within reach of his bony fingers, even when he slept.

Any onlooker would have found it impossible to tell whether he was asleep or awake because the infamous bounty hunter never closed his bullet-coloured eyes. He just remained perfectly still propped against the wall.

He would remain motionless until his honed instincts warned him that someone was close.

Only then would Iron Eyes move again.

8

It was a shuffling noise outside the shack which alerted Iron Eyes that someone was close and getting closer. Within a split second his bony hands had grabbed at both the matched pair of guns and drawn them on to his lap. His eyes darted to the door and stared. It was the stare an eagle would use when watching its grounded prey from a high thermal. It was focused and as sharp as a straight razor.

The sound grew closer.

It was that of feet.

Someone was coming towards the shack.

Iron Eyes went to move but agonizing pain tore through his weary body like the blade of a Bowie knife. He fell backwards until his spine was once more resting against the wooden wall of the shack. The bounty hunter felt helpless. He glanced at the Navy Colts in his hands. The last thing he ought to do was fire his guns. That would bring what was left of Fontaine's men down on him like vultures on a fresh carcass, he shrewdly thought.

If anyone were to enter the shack, the sensible thing he should do was dispose of the critter quietly. Either with the grip of one of his guns or anything else that was heavy enough to crush a skull.

Yet Iron Eyes was as stiff as a board and soaked in his own sweat. He was feverish. He only had the guns.

His mind raced.

Ted Cooper had told him that he finished work at the saloon at seven. The sun was still high outside the shack, its fiery light still visible through the sacking drapes. It was still only half-way through the afternoon, he calculated. No later than three or four. Whoever it was coming toward the shack, it was not the friendly bartender.

The feet were definitely getting closer.

74

Who was it?

Iron Eyes strained to hear.

His fevered mind knew that the footsteps were not that of a young person. They were the feet of someone either old or lame. They slid across the hard ground instead of lifting between steps. The bounty hunter gritted his teeth and felt the cigar fall from his mouth on to his shirt.

He had bitten right through it just as he had almost done with the bullet-casing earlier.

This was a new experience for Iron Eyes. He had never been unable to get to his feet before.

He did not like the experience.

Sweat dripped from his matted hair.

Iron Eyes tried to move again, and failed.

He was stiff. Every sinew in his lean body seemed to have locked up and refused to respond. His leg no longer hurt, yet he knew that it was the cause of all his problems. Maybe he had not managed to get all the glass out of the wound before he put the red-hot poker on to his torn flesh.

Could that have been why he was feverish?

Iron Eyes licked his dry lips and listened to the noise which grew louder to his trained hunting instincts. How many thousands of animals had he heard move towards him over the years as he lay in deadly wait?

Yet he had been agile then, unlike now.

Now he was stuck like a crippled deer caught in a trap.

Pain burned through him. It seemed to be moving around his body like a wave.

More sweat dripped from his head. He was confused. The last time he had felt this way he had been bitten by a rattler. The leg throbbed. He glanced at the wound. It was hideous. His only consolation was that the bleeding had stopped. His eyes glanced at the earthen floor. He knew that it had soaked up at least a quarter of his blood before he had managed to seal the deep wound.

The trapped man blew the long, wet hair off his face and continued to stare at the door. He raised both guns and trained them at the ill-fitting shack door. His hands started to shake as if unable to cope with the lightweight weapons in his grip.

Iron Eyes was even more confused.

What was happening to him?

His eyes darted down at the shaking guns in his hands.

What was happening to him? his brain asked again and again.

Then he heard a voice.

It was a woman's voice. An old woman's voice.

'Teddy? Are ya in there, son?'

The door started to be pushed inward. Iron Eyes lowered the guns which had started to feel like lead weights. He rested them on his lap and waited.

'Teddy? I seen the smoke. What ya doin' home so early?'

She was tiny. Less than five feet in height. At least six inches less. Her frame was buckled as so many old women's frames were when they reached a certain age. Her hair was white like snow and her face weathered by at least seventy years of existence. A shawl covered her shoulders and she carried a small basket in her left hand.

At first she did not seem to notice that the man on her son's bed was not her son. She slid one foot ahead of another until she reached half-way into the shack. Then she stopped and looked at Iron Eyes.

The bounty hunter could see that the pupils of both her eyes were white. She was half-blind.

'That ain't you is it, Teddy?' she asked feebly.

'I'm his friend,' Iron Eyes said in a low drawl.

Her head tilted. Iron Eyes could see that she was vainly straining to see who had spoken to her. Her feet shuffled a little as she tried to maintain her balance. It was like looking at a toddler who had just learned how to remain upright, he thought.

Life, if lived long enough, turns full circle.

'Teddy never said that anyone was comin' here, mister,' she said before carefully making her way to the only chair in the small structure. 'I thought that it was strange. Teddy never comes home early. Them folks who own the saloon keep him workin' all hours for a pittance.'

'Does Fontaine own the saloon?' Iron Eyes asked.

'Reckon so, young 'un. He owns everythin'. Damn crook.' She lowered her ancient frame down on to the chair and gave out a sigh of relief. 'Who are ya, boy?'

'My names Iron Eyes.'

'Injun?'

'Nope.'

'Damn Injuns killed my brother.' She sighed.

'Folks around here don't seem to like

Fontaine, do they?'

She smiled. It was a beautiful smile. Her looks had long since faded into history and her teeth were worn down, but the bounty hunter could still see what she had once been. A spark still burned in her spirited frame.

'Ain't it no wonder? That man came in here and just took over. His sort always do. I've seen his kind many times over the years. They just come in and steal everythin', Iron Eyes.'

Iron Eyes went to sit forward but pain forced him to remain exactly where he was. He gave out a gasp.

'Ya hurt, ain't ya?' she said firmly.

'Yep!' Iron Eyes admitted. 'I had me a run-in with a lot of Fontaine's hired guns, ma'am.'

'They shoot ya?' She seemed concerned.

'No, ma'am. But they sure tried.'

'What's wrong with ya then?' Her head kept moving as her eyes vainly attempted to see.

'I had to throw myself through a

window.' Iron Eyes sighed as he gently rubbed his leg. 'It was closed at the time. I managed to get a chunk of the glass in my leg.'

'Ya need a doctor?'

'Nope. I tended myself, ma'am.' Iron Eyes felt hot. Hotter than he should have felt. Sweat had soaked every stitch of his clothing. 'I just got me a real strange feelin'. I've got a fever, I reckon. Must have bin the glass. Must have bin dirty or somethin'.'

The old woman rose carefully. She opened up the basket and looked inside it. She tutted and then squinted at him.

'Ya needs mould,' she said. 'Mouldy cheese or bread or the likes. Mould can break a fever. Don't know how or why, but it does.'

'Mould? Ain't that poison?' the bounty hunter queried. 'I don't wanna eat nothin' that's poisonous, ma'am. Thanks all the same.'

She shuffled toward the door.

'Don't ya go arguin' with old Bessie Cooper, boy. My ma always said that mould could break a fever. Ya don't wanna go callin' my ma a liar, do ya?'

'I'm too tuckered to argue, ma'am.'

'Good! I might be old but I can still look after myself!' She muttered. 'Stay there! I'll make ya better!'

'Where ya goin'?' Iron Eyes asked.

'To get some mouldy bread from my larder!' she replied. 'My shack's only a few yards from here! You stay put! Right! That's an order!'

Iron Eyes watched as she went back out into the sunlight. He rested the back of his head against the wooden wall and exhaled.

'OK, Bessie Cooper. I reckon you'd win if we tussled.'

9

The afternoon sun was falling across the fertile grassland range on its daily descent to signal to the multitude of creatures below its fiery orb that night was only an hour or so away. The swaying grass which belied the arid deserts that dominated most of the vast territory continued to feed the thousands of steers as it had done since the first pioneers discovered this Eden, in a territory that some claimed had been created by the Satan himself. Red sheets of cloud whispers hung across the blue sky as the blazing sun headed earthward the same way it had done since time began. The buildings of Hope seemed bathed in a crimson paint that only the devil would have chosen from his fiery palette.

The innocent men and women who lived within the boundaries of the sun-bleached town felt that it might be an omen. They had already seen the stranger battle against Brewster Fontaine's men in deadly combat. For the first time they had witnessed someone actually getting the better of Fontaine's army of hired gunmen.

In a few minutes Iron Eyes had proved that Fontaine was not invincible. The residents of Hope at last had a glimmer of that precious emotion coursing through their veins again. The name of the town had long been an irony.

Now it was real and Fontaine was not oblivious to the fact.

The last thing he wanted was a mutiny amongst the people he had controlled for so many years. He was worried and it showed across his handsome carved features.

He had to assert his power over them once again, and do it fast. There was no room for complacency. He was well aware that the hundreds of honest men living in the town and its neighbours outnumbered his deadly army. If they rediscovered the courage of which he had brutally stripped them, no amount of hired killers could stop them.

Fontaine sat amid twenty of his gunmen in the very centre of the Spinning Wheel. A handful of towns-people whom he did not employ fringed the walls, downing their beer and whiskey.

The Hope businessman ensured that the table where he brooded was surrounded by his men. He had his back well covered should anyone suddenly get ambitious.

Then it happened.

One of the drinkers suddenly got loud. That was always a bad sign in any drinking- or gambling-hole. For some folks get deaf when they have con-sumed too much liquor. They also get a false sense of their own worth.

'Ya ain't lookin' so big now, Fon-taine!' the drunken man screamed out across the saloon. 'That scarecrow whooped ya ass real good! Ya lost a lotta men this afternoon, boy! Reckon ya gonna lose a lot more!'

The hired guns all turned and stared at the man who had risen to his feet and was swaying like a blade of long grass out on the range. He had a gunbelt strapped around his middle and his right hand rested on the grip of a gun he had long since lost the ability to use.

'What'll we do, boss?' one of the standing men called Big Harry asked.

Fontaine stared at the whiskey bottle which had less than three fingers of liquor remaining inside its clear moulded glass shape. Riley was to his left and Keno to his right.

'Shut his mouth up!' Fontaine replied without bothering to look at Big Harry.

The large gunman led the rest of the gunmen towards the shouting man.

'Stay back, ya bastards!' the drunken man shouted. 'I'll kill ya all if ya don't!'

'Easy, old-timer!' Big Harry said as he and his fellow gun hands continued to close in on the irate man. 'Ya liquored up and ain't in no fit state to kill no one!'

'Shut the hell up, Hyram!' one of the other seated men nervously said to the swaying man. 'Sit down before ya gets yaself killed! These boys get paid to kill the likes of us, and ya ain't no gunslinger! Sit down!'

'I ain't feared of no trail trash like this bunch, Joe!' the man slurred. 'I killed me a lotta critters like them in the old days! That scarecrow showed us how to kill these lily-livered bastards this afternoon! It ain't hard! Ya just draws and shoots!'

Then he decided to demonstrate. It was to be his last mistake in a life of many similar errors.

The drunken man hauled his gun from its holster and clawed with his thumb at the hammer. It had been a long time since he had attempted to do anything so foolhardy. The gun had not seen a drop of gun-oil in a decade. Its hammer was rigid with rust, as was its trigger.

That meant nothing to Fontaine's henchmen.

Big Harry drew and blasted a hole through the man named Hyram's midriff. Guts and blood splattered all over the wall behind the drunken man. Then the rest of the gunmen copied the deadly action. The acrid aroma of gunsmoke choked the seated onlookers. The deafening roar of gunfire shook the saloon's interior.

Before the body hit the floor another dozen bullets had torn him to shreds. The remaining men sat drinking around the corpse and stared in disbelief at the ferocity of the attack. They kept their hands on the tables before them so that the gunslingers would not turn their venom on them as well.

'What'll we do with this, boss?' Big Harry asked through the clouds of gunsmoke that swirled around the saloon as he pointed at the body.

'Throw it out front with the rest of the garbage, Harry,' Fontaine muttered.

'The undertaker will take care of it!'

Big Harry touched the brim of his hat and waved at the closest four of the gunmen. The quartet of gunmen grabbed the blood-soaked body by its arms and feet and carried it across the floor towards the swing-doors. A trail of blood marked their route over the sawdust.

They unceremoniously tossed what was left of the drunk's body out on to the sand between the hitching-rails. The horses shied away from the smell and sight of death. Only their leather reins secured to the rails prevented them from galloping away in terror.

The henchmen walked back into the Spinning Wheel and resumed their places around their paymaster.

Fontaine looked to either side of him at Keno and Riley and cleared his throat. They continued to talk and drink. 'Remind me, what do I pay you boys for?'

'Killin' folks!' Riley answered.

'Then why didn't ya get up and kill

that drunk?' Fontaine hissed like a snake.

'What drunk?' Riley joked.

Keno leaned forward and rested both elbows on the table. He glanced at Fontaine hard.

'What's wrong, boss? We lost men before and ya didn't get yaself all worked up then! What's different?'

'Where could Iron Eyes have gone?' Fontaine asked for the hundredth time. 'Men can't just disappear like that into thin air! Where did Iron Eyes go?'

Riley held the thimble glass in his left hand and gazed at the amber liquid in it. He downed the whiskey and then placed the glass back down on to the table.

'We'll get the varmint!' he slurred. 'Ain't no way that he'll manage to get out of this town without one of the boys noticing, boss. I sent Clem to call in every one of our boys from around the range. They'll be here before midnight!'

Keno poured himself and Riley another drink from the bottle.

'Frank's right, boss. Iron Eyes must be wounded 'coz ya found his blood out there on the boardwalk. I figure he's curled up underneath one of them boardwalks waiting to die!'

Fontaine sighed.

'That's the liquor talking, Keno! Iron Eyes might be wounded but his sort don't just curl up and wait to die! His sort tries to take as many folks as he can with him to hell! Nope, I reckon that bounty hunter is hiding to get the drop on the rest of us!'

Riley glanced at his boss.

'I've got the rest of the boys huntin' that bastard! If he's anywhere in Hope they'll find him, boss! Stop frettin'!'

'I ain't frettin', Riley!' Fontaine snarled. 'I'm just not used to havin' someone loose in town that's as good as he is with his guns! He's already slaughtered almost a third of my men! He could strike at any time at any place! I don't cotton to folks that hit what they're aimin' at, Riley! He might aim his guns at me!'

'Maybe ya should have paid him the bounty money,' Keno suggested. 'He sure got worked up when he realized that ya wasn't gonna let him get his hands on that reward money!'

'Iron Eyes must be loco!' Riley growled. 'No sane *hombre* would have gone up against so many guns! Yep! Iron Eyes must be plumb loco!'

Walt Jason, another of Fontaine's hired guns, walked through the swing-doors of the saloon and ambled across the sawdust towards Fontaine's table. The young gunslinger pulled out a telegraph message from his vest-pocket and handed it to his boss.

'The telegraph operator gave me this for ya, boss!' Jason said, gazing around at the blood which covered the floor and wall.

Fontaine unfolded the paper and read the brief message. His eyes widened as he absorbed the words.

'Damn it all! If I ain't got enough troubles! Now this!'

'What's wrong, boss?' Keno asked.

'Looks like we got us company headed this way!' Fontaine said in a heavy voice. 'A certain Herbert Carmichael has been sent here from Washington to try and steal our territory out from under us. He wants to turn old Arizona into another state! If that happens I'll be ruined!'

The faces of the two gunmen seated on either side of Fontaine suddenly went pale. Every hired gun who roamed the territories knew what would happen once statehood took over.

'We can't allow that critter to pull the rug out from under us, boss!' Keno said urgently.

'We have to stop him!' Riley added.

'I know!' Fontaine agreed. 'The trouble is that Carmichael has himself a military escort. Anything we do will be reported back East. It might ricochet in our faces if we just kill them. The government might decide to send in a hundred times as many troopers with another Carmichael! There has to be another way!'

'What can we do?' Keno asked. 'I reckon we just ought to kill them all and see what happens!'

'Keno's right, boss!' Riley nodded.

'We have to kill him and his escort in a way that will make them Eastern dudes think that this is one territory that's just too wild to be tamed just yet!' Fontaine replied. 'But how are we going to do that?'

'What if we ambush him and make it look like it's Injuns on the warpath?' Riley suggested. 'If we got all the boys together and dressed up like redskins, we could attack them! Them Easterners don't cotton to Injuns!'

'That might work!' Fontaine nodded in agreement. 'They might swallow that one if we did it right! They ain't to know that there ain't an Indian within fifty miles of here! We kill just enough of them to make them turn tail and run! That way the news will get back East fast! They might just think that Arizona is still too wild to become a state!'

'It might work!' Keno shrugged.

'What about Iron Eyes?' Riley asked Fontaine. 'We ain't caught him yet, boss!'

'Iron Eyes can wait!' Fontaine stood and threw the telegraph message at the floor. 'First we have to bushwhack this Carmichael critter!'

Fontaine led his men out of the saloon to where their horses were tied to the hitching-rails. Ted Cooper polished a beer-glass and silently watched from behind the bar counter as the deadly hired killers mounted their horses and rode in the direction of Fontaine's house.

He had heard every word.

Whoever this Carmichael was, the bartender thought, he was in trouble. Real big trouble.

The wall clock started to chime across the room. His eyes glanced at it and saw that it was seven. Slim Parker, his relief bartender entered the Spinning Wheel.

'Howdy, Ted!' Parker said as he

started to unwrap his white apron. 'Reckon ya ready to go home, huh?'

Cooper removed his apron, then picked up his coat from under the counter. He slipped it on.

'Yeah! It's bin a real strange day, Slim!' Cooper said.

Parker paused and looked at the bloody sawdust and the human debris covering the wall behind the quiet drinkers.

'Who got shot?'

'Hyram!' Cooper shrugged. 'He got himself liquored up and Fontaine had his boys shut him up permanent!'

'I'd better get a bucket of soapy water and wash this mess down before it starts to stink the saloon out!' Slim Parker sighed.

'See ya!' Cooper patted the shoulder of his pal and headed for the rear door leading to the back alleys which stretched from one end of Hope to the other. He entered the shadows and glanced up at the red sky. He started walking. He knew the alleys would take him back to his small shack and the guest he had sent there hours earlier. He was also thankful that he had brushed away all evidence of the bleeding bounty hunter's departure. If any of Fontaine's men had spotted the trail of blood they would have followed.

With every step Cooper wondered if Iron Eyes could possibly still be alive. The pitifully thin bounty hunter had been pumping blood the last time he had seen him. The bartender knew that unless the flow of blood had been stopped, there was no chance of Iron Eyes having survived since he had last seen him.

Was it possible for him to have survived this long?

No normal human being could have, yet was the monstrous Iron Eyes actually human? He appeared more like a monster than anything created in his Maker's image!

Cooper quickened his pace. He recalled the horrific face of the bounty hunter. Iron Eyes had looked more dead than alive even before he had been wounded.

The high fences shielded Cooper from prying eyes, just as they had hidden the strange rider when he galloped away from the back of the saloon.

Cooper knew it would soon be dark.

It could not come too soon for the nervous bartender.

10

Territorial Governor John Masterson was an honourable soul of honest conviction. Unfortunately the man who had been sent from Washington DC to act as his secretary had no such virtue. Herbert Carmichael had lived his entire adult life trying to make America not only bigger, but better. It was also an ambition he had designated for himself. Few unelected men in government had grown as prosperous as Carmichael himself. He had entered the civil service as a twenty-five-year-old straight out of college and achieved a meteoric rise to success. Carmichael had learned early how to manipulate the rules which governed politics. Rules were made to be bent to one's advantage, and he had no equal when it came to such matters. He had grown wealthy far beyond what his salary should have allowed, yet there were few in Washington DC who would have dared question the integrity of their peers. When you live in glass houses, it is never wise to throw stones. Even his enemies knew that you never pointed an accusing finger at anyone, for fear it might seek you out next.

Carmichael had been quicker than most of his contemporaries to realize the financial possibilities of exploiting the expanding West, and how someone in his position could profit from encouraging it.

For years he had tried to turn every available territory into a new state, whatever the cost. He was a single-minded soul who had little truck with those who had sympathy for the Indians who had once occupied the vast land beyond the Appalachians. Tribe after tribe were cast aside to satisfy his ambition. To the ignorant Easterners the Indians were nothing but savages. They deserved no favours from the superior white man.

He knew how to exploit the fears of

his fellow man, how to get them to turn a blind eye to any atrocities. It was something which came naturally to the majority of them. At least a third of the senators had at one time owned slaves.

The heart of America was a land that Carmichael considered the perfect place to send the East coast's surplus population.

Turn a territory into a state and you could tax the majority who clawed out an existence there. Carmichael had many friends who would tender their bids to him for government contracts to 'tame' the wilderness with the knowledge that they would be successful.

Carmichael always granted contracts to those companies that had been generous to him. For nearly thirty years he had learned how to work the system. It did not matter to him who was crushed underfoot in the process.

There was not a single sympathetic bone in fifty-four-year-old Carmichael's body. To him, it was just business. Dirty business, but business all the same. He was no better or worse than the rest of his kind.

He was just a lot shrewder.

Secretary Carmichael saw the financial possibilities that expansion could bring, not just to the government, but mainly to himself. He was no better than the territories' criminals whom he had publicly vowed to cast out and destroy.

At least the gamblers, conmen and killers who had been driven into one territory after another, fleeing civilization, had been brave enough to risk their lives in their pursuit of riches.

Carmichael, however, hid behind the flag and pretended to be patriotic.

In truth, he was just another thief.

Once again Carmichael had managed to convince the authorities back East that he was the man for the job of helping Governor Masterson bring civilization to yet another massive chunk of American acreage. The job of convincing the people within another territory that joining the Union and embracing statehood would be good for them was something at which he had already been successful. Carmichael would omit telling any of them that once Arizona became a state, it would come under the control of faceless bureaucrats thousands of miles away.

Freedom as they had known it would no longer exist.

Herbert Carmichael had a lot riding on success in his latest mission. He had already accepted the advance gifts and money the tenderers had showered on him upon his agreeing that he would ensure their bids were on top of the pile when the government contracts were dished out.

All he had to do now was get Arizona to go, unwittingly, along with his proposals.

As always when he entered lawless territories, Carmichael was escorted by a troop of well-armed cavalry. No fewer than forty of the seasoned Seventh had flanked either side of his carriage all the way from Fort Bragg.

He sat inside his handsome conveyance with his only child, Florence for company. The nineteen-year-old had no idea why she had been enlisted to accompany her father on this important visit. She assumed, as most loving children do, that her father was proud of her and wanted to show her off. Florence was indeed a beautiful female.

In truth, the heartless Carmichael wanted his daughter as nothing more than a human shield. She would be sacrificed if the need arose. He knew that even the most ruthless of outlaws would rarely fire a gun at their worst enemies if a handsome female was close at hand.

Women were far too scarce in the Wild West. To risk shooting one by accident was unthinkable.

The vehicle that Carmichael had commissioned to be built was not what it appeared to be. From the outside it looked as though it was of wooden construction. The carriage was in fact made of cast iron and had been covered with a thin veneer of wooden panels. It weighed three times as much as an ordinary stagecoach. Six sturdy horses were required to pull its immense weight, and even then the animals could barely cover twenty miles in a day.

Carmichael had planned their route and ensured that on each night of their long overland journey he and his escort would take refuge in one of the many stagecoach way stations which were dotted across the vast desert and plains.

Captain Bob Sherwood led his troop and the hefty well-armoured carriage down through a dusty draw into the flat plains toward the Overland Stage Company outpost at Apache Wells. The sun was low. Sherwood knew that the six-horse team was again exhausted from pulling the massive vehicle.

Carmichael watched from inside the carriage with a satisfied smile upon his face. He could see the flaming torches on the high-walled way station, indicating that darkness would soon be with them again. Tomorrow they would reach the fertile range filled with a multitude of cattle. A jewel in the crown of the mainly arid territory.

He knew the risks that he faced when he eventually reached his destination. They were formidable. There were always scores of wealthy men who wanted nothing to do with relinquishing their hold on what they believed was theirs.

They would do anything to stop him.

This was why he travelled inside a bullet-proof carriage.

But even though the risks were immense, Carmichael knew the rewards made it all worthwhile.

Carmichael had accepted far too many bribes for this venture to fail. There was no way that he would have even considered paying back all the dirty money he had accumulated. He had to succeed. There was no other option.

Yet if he had known anything of Brewster Fontaine he might have not been quite so eager to reach the settlement of Hope. He might have realized that his military escort was barely half the strength of Fontaine's hired army of guns.

As the carriage and forty cavalrymen entered the way station's compound, Carmichael knew that he was less than twenty-four hours away from lush grassland.

The final leg of their perilous journey was almost upon them.

Only a hearty meal and a good night's sleep lay between them and a fate which had yet to be devised in the ruthless minds of men who were quite as evil as himself.

11

A million twinkling stars hung over the sprawling town casting their eerie light over everything below. Iron Eyes had slept since eating the stale, mould-covered bread the old female had given him. For three hours Bessie Cooper had sat at the foot of the bed and listened to the tortured ramblings which spewed from the lips of her patient. Iron Eyes had fought against the fevered nightmares which had haunted him since he succumbed to the long overdue sleep.

The small shack was dark. Its only illumination came from the dim light that flickered from the wick inside the glass bowl of the battered oil-lantern on the table. Yet there might have well been no light at all. One of the shack's occupants was deep in sleep whilst the other had eyes which could barely tell night from day.

She wondered what the man who had been ravaged by fever for so many hours actually looked like. Everyone she met nowadays was merely a voice and a hazy outline of muted colour. Her ancient eyes could only see vague shapes which were masked by a milky film. Yet she had sensed something in his quiet, low voice that reminded her of another man. A man who had been her only true love and who had died more than twenty years earlier. A broken heart still ached inside her weary body.

Her life had been hard. Bessie had worked, as all pioneer wives did, in an unforgiving land. She had seen only one of her thirteen children live to beyond his tenth birthday. Teddy was all she had, and to her he was precious. Indians and illness had destroyed everything she had ever loved with the exception of her son.

Yet she did not complain.

Even crippled and getting blinder

with every passing day, there was nothing powerful enough to make this female seek refuge in self-pity.

Bessie was stronger than that.

She had sat patting the delirious bounty hunter's boot for hours since he had slipped into the deep sleep. A million memories flooded her mind. She had sat helplessly beside so many of her children until they had lost their individual battles with the Grim Reaper. Then it had been her husband's turn to be struck down in his prime.

So many unmarked graves filled her memory.

Yet she remained defiantly calm because even with eyes which could no longer see, the faces of all her cherished family still lived inside her mind.

Suddenly Bessie's attention was drawn from the helpless man on her son's bed to the door and what lay beyond it. She heard the familiar footsteps approaching the shack.

Bessie Cooper inhaled and smiled

as the door opened.

'Teddy!' she sighed.

'You OK, Ma?' Cooper asked as he leaned over and kissed her cheek. He stared at the sweat-soaked figure, then dragged the chair across the earthen floor and sat beside his mother. 'I see ya met my new pal.'

'He was hurt, Teddy,' Bessie said. 'He was burnin' up with fever so I give him some mouldy bread. He's bin sleepin' ever since.'

Cooper looked up and down the long emaciated figure. His gaze rested when he spotted the torn pants leg and the inflamed wound that Iron Eyes had burned into submission with the red-hot poker. The bartender gritted his teeth and shook his head.

'Ya reckon he'll pull through, Ma?'

'I don't rightly know, son.' She sighed, patting the boot once more. 'I think he's got a fifty-fifty chance. What's he do for a livin', boy?'

'He's a bounty hunter, Ma,' Cooper whispered. 'He took on Fontaine's best men and killed two dozen of the critters.'

She gasped.

'He did? But he seems so gentle. His voice is so peaceful. I think they must have picked on him! He don't seem the kinda man that starts trouble.'

Cooper smiled.

'That there man is as tough as they gets, Ma. His name's Iron Eyes!'

'I know his name, Teddy. He told me. I thought he was an Injun for a while.'

The bounty hunter inhaled deeply and rolled his head over. He was still muttering nonsense under his breath. 'He is a strange one, though. There ain't an ounce of meat on his bones. I can't figure how he ain't died of hunger.'

Cooper nodded.

'Damn right, Ma.'

'No cussin', Teddy!'

'Sorry,' Cooper apologized. 'I ought to make us a little grub. I figure we could all do with a full belly.'

Iron Eyes raised his right hand and

pushed the long sweat-soaked strands of hair off his face. His eyes adjusted to the dim light and then fixed on the two other occupants of the shack.

'What happened?' he asked in a low drawl.

Bessie leaned forward and patted his arm. She could not conceal her joy.

'Ya fever just broke, boy,' she announced joyously. 'Ya fever broke.'

Cooper walked from the stove to the bed. He looked down at the confused bounty hunter.

'How'd ya feel, Iron Eyes?'

'Better than I did, Ted.'

'Teddy's gonna fix us some vittles!' Bessie said. 'He can cook up a feast out of thin air. When you've had somethin' to eat, you'll feel a heck of a lot better.'

Iron Eyes propped himself up on one elbow and looked at Cooper.

'They still lookin' for me, Ted?' he asked.

Cooper pushed more kindling into the stove.

'They found themselves a bigger

target, Iron Eyes! A government dude from back East. Some critter named Carmichael that's bin sent to try and persuade the folks in Arizona to vote for statehood! That has to be a dude headed for Boot Hill and no mistake!'

'Fontaine must be mighty afraid of losin' his grip on this territory.' Iron Eyes sighed.

'More than afraid, Iron Eyes,' Ted said. 'He's terrified of losin' his fortune! Everythin' he's got is tied up in this territory! His sort ain't worth a plugged nickel outside Arizona!'

'Are ya sure that they're gonna kill this Carmichael dude?' The bounty hunter was curious.

'Yep! I heard them talkin' in the Spinnin' Wheel. Fontaine and his boys are gonna dress up as Injuns and attack Carmichael's coach.' Cooper repeated the information that he had overheard in the saloon. 'It's got a military escort, but they're gonna ambush it anyways!'

'As long as they stop huntin' my hide for a while, I don't care!' Iron Eyes said.

'I still ain't got my bounty money though, and that makes it darn hard to just ride out of here!'

'Ya ain't still gonna try and get that money, is ya?' Cooper gasped.

'Yep!' Iron Eyes nodded. 'I earned it and a whole lot more if ya tally up the bounty on them dead gunslingers. I reckon every single one of them was wanted dead or alive.'

'But they'll kill ya!'

Iron Eyes shook his head.

'So ya said that they've forgotten all about killin' me, Ted Cooper!'

Cooper picked up a skillet and placed it on top of the stove. Then he turned.

'Nope! They intend killin' you after they've killed Carmichael!'

Iron Eyes sat up.

'Reckon I'd better do somethin' about that!' he drawled. Cooper stared in disbelief at the bounty hunter.

'Are ya loco?'

'When ya got a bunch of gunslingers on ya trail, ya gotta do somethin', Ted,' Iron Eyes explained. 'Ya gotta turn on them first! They started this war, but I'll finish it!'

'After ya vittles, boy!' Bessie waved a finger. 'Ya ain't doin' nothin' until ya belly is full! Savvy?'

Iron Eyes nodded to the blind female and then touched her cheek softly.

'Sure, ma'am! I savvy!'

12

The large livery stable was set well away from the town's main street. Its aroma hung heavily on the warm night air. The tall wooden structure had seen better days, as had its hard-working owner, Will Hume. The brawny blacksmith still had plenty of muscles, but now his once impressive frame was dominated by a huge swollen belly which hid his wide black leather belt. Hume seldom closed the large doors for business. He could not afford to turn any work away, whatever time of the day or night it came.

Hume lived in a small room set to the righthand side of the livery stable's frontage. His life was little more than a constant wait. He was always waiting for someone to bring their mounts to him, to either look after for the night, or to replace horseshoes.

If he was lucky he might see a dozen silver dollars in a week.

It was nearly ten and the town's back streets were quiet apart from the occasional sound of a tinny piano carried on the night breeze from the closest of the towns saloons. Few men ventured to this part of Hope unless they were collecting their mounts from the livery stable.

The street was lit by a single coal-tar lantern perched on a high pole fifty yards from the front of the large building. Its light did not reach the wide-open doors. To the right of the stable was a corral. This was also owned by the blacksmith.

Hume munched with what teeth he had left inside his mouth on a dry chunk of bread as he inspected the half-dozen horses tied up in their stalls.

The flickering light from two oil-lanterns hanging on chains suspended from the rafters gave the interior of the stable a strange haunting illumination. Black shadows seemed to dance to the tune created by the light of the flaming kerosene-soaked wicks.

To the more imaginative it might have seemed as if demons or the like were possessing the cavernous structure, but the blacksmith had stopped believing in ghosts long ago. He knew that such things were for the weak-minded. There was only the reality of a life which had grown harder and harder to survive.

The eyes of the horses in the stalls sparkled as Hume checked each in turn.

The blacksmith might have been long past his best days, but he was good at his job. No horse that he cared for ever lacked attention, food or water.

Even in his darkest moments the burly man never allowed his own despair to affect his work. Hume never mistreated any animals in his stables. He knew that however bad his life had become, their burden was far heavier than his own.

After checking the last of the horses,

the well-built Hume nodded in satisfaction and made to return to his small living-quarters to finish his supper.

Suddenly he sensed that he was no longer alone inside the large building.

He paused and looked around.

For a moment he saw nothing. Then his eyes focused on the shape of a tall figure framed in the middle of the stable's open doors.

The sight startled the blacksmith.

Hume took a backward step and tried to focus even harder on the unexpected visitor. He told himself that whatever this creature was, it had to be human. The trouble was, no human had ever put the fear of God into him the way this apparition did. Hume felt his heart pounding inside his broad chest. His throat felt as if a noose had been tightened around it.

The blacksmith steadied himself and swallowed hard. He rubbed his whiskered chin with the palms of his hands and forced himself to step forward once again. The light from the pair of lanterns caught the metal of a pair of Navy Colt gun grips which poked out from the man's belt.

Iron Eyes remained totally still.

Only his long limp hair moved as the gentle breeze washed over his broad shoulders from along the empty street. Hume had not heard the tall skeletal figure approaching. Even with an injured leg, Iron Eyes's honed hunting instincts had not deserted him. He was still able to move unseen and unheard when he had to.

'Ya open for business?' Iron Eyes asked.

'I'm always open for business, stranger!'

'Good!'

'Who are ya?' Hume asked nervously.

'My name's Iron Eyes!'

Hume gasped.

'The bounty hunter?'

Iron Eyes nodded.

'Yep!'

13

Fear fuelled the imagination of Will Hume as he stared open-mouthed at the unholy image of Iron Eyes bathed in the blackest of the livery stable's shadows. He knew that the infamous bounty hunter had a thousand ways of killing. Each and every one of them flashed through his mind. The black-smith could feel his knees knocking as the tall figure limped toward him silently. The chilling realization that the most hunted man in Hope was less than a few yards away from him made Hume feel as if he were living his last moments on earth.

If death had a face, then surely this was it.

As Iron Eyes ventured into the light of one of the suspended lanterns Hume gave a gasp. He had never seen anyone who looked like the tall man before. A hundred or more battles were carved into the features of the bounty hunter. Scars twisted the flesh of Iron Eyes' face until it no longer looked remotely human. The small bullet-coloured eyes peered rapidly all around the interior of the large stable as if seeking out enemies yet to be discovered.

The grips of the well-used guns poked out from the belt around the thin belly of the bounty hunter. The blacksmith knew that at any moment the bony hands might drag them from the belt and start dishing out their own brand of justice — 36-calibre justice.

Iron Eyes' infamous legend had reached this remote town long before he had physically appeared.

Hume licked his dry lips and tried to speak. His throat was too tight to allow even a single word to pass between them. Again his eyes were drawn to the pair of matched Navy Colts pushed into Iron Eyes' pants' belt. Their grips jutted out defiantly at the blacksmith as he limped toward the horses.

'I need me a horse!' Iron Eyes said bluntly. 'Nothin' fancy. Just an animal that can gallop until it drops and ain't frightened of gunplay!'

Hume turned slowly and attempted to compose himself.

'Two of these nags belong to townsfolk. The others are mine. Take ya pick.'

Iron Eyes looked up and down the stalled mounts.

'Which one is the best?'

'The grey,' Hume answered quickly. 'He's the most reliable when it comes to bein' sure-footed!'

Iron Eyes limped to the grey horse and stared at it coldly. He had never liked horses and yet found that they were the one thing he could not do without.

'How much?'

'F-forty dollars.' Hume stammered nervously. He was too scared to ask more, even though he knew that the grey was probably worth double. 'Is that OK?'

'Fine!' Iron Eyes muttered.

Hume felt a little less frightened. Then a thought suddenly occurred to him.

'How did ya get here without me hearing ya, Iron Eyes?' he asked innocently.

'A friend gave me a ride up to ya corral. I limped the rest of the way.'

'But I never heard them spurs of yours make even the smallest of noises!' Hume pointed at the large spurs attached to the mule-eared boots. 'I don't get it!'

'They're kinda rusted up with blood!' the bounty hunter responded quietly. 'Horse blood!'

'Oh!' Hume gulped.

Iron Eyes glanced at the blacksmith again. This time his eyes were narrowed and seemed to have fire in their blazing gaze.

'Ya ain't seen my saddle and bags, have ya? My horse was shot earlier today outside the saloon.'

Without a second's hesitation Hume

125

nodded his head slowly and pointed to the corner. The saddle and bridle were there with the saddle-bags on top of a bale of hay.

'There! I had to use a wagon to drag ya horse here from the Spinning Wheel after that gunfight. I buried it out back. I put all ya gear over there. I never opened the bags.'

Iron Eyes said nothing.

He limped to the pile of his only possessions, plucked up the bags off the saddle and opened both satchels. He studied the contents carefully. His eyes then returned to the nervous blacksmith.

'What's ya name?'

'Will Hume,' the blacksmith replied.

'Ya an honest man, Will Hume. Damn honest.' Iron Eyes said.

Hume felt as if a weight had been lifted from his powerful shoulders. For the first time since encountering the strange figure, he felt that Iron Eyes had no intention of killing him. He watched as the bounty hunter slowly limped back towards him with the bags over his left forearm.

'Ya must have seen the golden eagles in my bag?' Iron Eyes queried before adding: 'Most men could not have resisted that kinda temptation.'

'I told ya. I never looked,' Hume said. 'I figured that ya would come back for ya goods if'n ya lived long enough. And by the looks of all them bodies that was stacked up on main street, I reckoned you was mighty hard to kill.'

'I still say that ya honest!'

'Reckon so!'

Iron Eyes held out his hand and offered two fifty-dollar gold pieces to the blacksmith. They glinted in the lantern-light.

Hume looked at them and shrugged.

'I ain't got me any money, Iron Eyes. I can't break even one gold piece.'

Iron Eyes leaned closer and pushed the coins into the man's vest-pocket.

'Keep them. Ya earned the difference.'

Hume's face lit up.

'I thought ya was gonna kill me.' He sighed heavily.

Iron Eyes nodded.

'I would have killed ya if ya'd stolen my money, Will Hume!'

The blacksmith shuddered.

'I knew being honest would pay off one day!'

Iron Eyes draped the saddle-bags over the top of the stall rail and ran a hand down the neck of the grey. His mind was racing as he tried to work out how he could get the better of Brewster Fontaine and lay his hands on the reward money that was due to him. He also thought about the information that Ted Cooper had given him about the government man called Carmichael.

Iron Eyes had always tried to stay on the right side of the law, but in this town and territory it was a mighty thin line between right and wrong. He knew that if Carmichael had the full power of the law behind him it might be profitable to locate him and his army escort. This man could get Iron Eyes his bounty money if anyone could.

Iron Eyes watched as the blacksmith released the rope across the stall where the grey stood.

'Tell me, if someone was headed here by stagecoach, which way would they come, Will?'

'Ain't no stages ever comes here, Iron Eyes,' the blacksmith said as he led the grey out of its stall. 'This town is just too dangerous for them stage-coach owners to risk it. We got us a town full of outlaws and that don't sit well with them folks.'

'But if they did, which route would they take?' Iron Eyes knew that there had to be a trail for merchant traders to bring goods to Hope and the other towns that fringed the fertile grassland.

Hume paused.

'East of here Apache Wells has a way station,' he told the tall figure. 'I heard that they was thinkin' of branchin' down here one day, but so far they ain't. The Overland Stage Company uses that place to change teams and feed their passengers, I'm told. That's gotta be the closest route to Hope, I guess.'

'That's gotta be it!' Iron Eyes said.

'Gotta be what?' Hume asked as he threw a blanket on the back of the grey and patted it down.

'The place that Fontaine will be headed toward with his men!'

Hume looked confused.

'What ya talkin' about, Iron Eyes? Why would Fontaine head over there?'

Iron Eyes shrugged.

'It's a long story. I heard that he was gonna attack some folks. Folks from the East that wanna try and turn this territory into a state.'

'Ya gonna go help them folks?' Hume asked. He walked across the livery to the saddle and lifted it up.

'Nope. I'm gonna warn them. That's different,' Iron Eyes corrected as Hume returned with the saddle.

'Ya don't seem the sort to go stickin' ya nose into other folks' troubles.' The blacksmith hauled the saddle on top of the blanket on the grey's back.

'I ain't!' Iron Eyes said bluntly. 'I'm gonna make sure that the authorities get my side of the story before this Fontaine critter has me branded as a killer!'

Hume reached below the horse's belly and gathered up the cinch straps. He threaded them through their buckles and looked over the saddle at the bounty hunter.

'So ya ain't gonna help them folks at Apache Wells, huh?'

'I'm gonna make sure that I get my bounty money!' Iron Eyes explained. 'I'm owed, Will. I'm owed a lot!'

The blacksmith's strong arms tightened and secured the cinch straps. For some reason he did not believe the bounty hunter. It seemed to him that Iron Eyes just could not prevent himself from finding new battles to fight.

'What if Fontaine does attack them Eastern folks?' he asked. 'Are ya tryin' to tell me that ya won't help kill Fontaine and his gang?'

Iron Eyes gave a slight grin.

'Come to think of it, killin' Fontaine and that bunch of killers might be profitable at that, Will.' The bounty hunter sighed.

'Ya a mighty strange man, Iron Eyes!' Hume declared. 'Ain't killin' just killin'?'

'Nope! I never kill anyone who ain't got bounty on their heads!' Iron Eyes answered. 'Killin' folks who ain't wanted dead or alive is just a waste of bullets, and I hate wasting bullets! There ain't no profit in that!'

Hume watched Iron Eyes drape the saddle-bags behind the cantle and secure them with leather laces. Then the bounty hunter carefully mounted the grey and gathered up the reins.

'Where ya headed first? To Apache Wells?'

'First I have to see what Fontaine and his boys are doing! I have to make sure that they are gonna head for Apache Wells and that Carmichael varmint! If they are, then I have to ride and warn them people!'

'What ya think will happen, Iron Eyes?'

Iron Eyes gave a wry smile.

'Well, Will, if things stack up the way they usually do, I'm headed straight into the jaws of death! The question is, will it be mine or the bastards that keep shootin' at me?'

Before the blacksmith could respond the spurs jabbed into the flesh of the grey. The startled animal leapt into action. Iron Eyes rode out into the dark street. Hume ran to the large, open stable doors, but there was no sign of either the horse or its new master.

Like the mythical phantoms he so resembled, Iron Eyes had vanished into the blackness of the night.

'I'd hate to be any of the folks loco enough to try and stop that critter!' Hume whispered to himself. 'That *hombre*'s a sack of rattlers!'

14

Like a bat out of hell Iron Eyes
thundered along the back streets
towards the large building which lay on
the outskirts of Hope. The building
which he knew was Brewster Fontaine's
magnificent home. The grey was as
good as the blacksmith had claimed. Its
hoofs ate up the ground in response to
the bounty hunter's silent commands.

Iron Eyes whipped the animal's
shoulders with the long ends of his
reins and spurred. There was no time to
lose. He had to find out whether Ted
Cooper had heard correctly. The
bounty hunter had to find out if
Fontaine and what remained of his
army of outlaws were going to mas-
querade as Indians and attack the way
station at Apache Wells.

The injured bounty hunter knew that
there was only one certain way to

discover the truth. He had somehow to get into the house or its grounds and find out the truth for himself.

But there was no way that he could approach the house from the front. That would be suicidal if all of Fontaine's henchmen were there. This was a job which could only be done by using the shadows.

The narrow street came to an abrupt end. Iron Eyes hauled on his reins and stopped the powerful animal beneath his saddle. The grey spun around as its master studied the fences and backs of buildings. Then he saw a lane. Instinctively Iron Eyes knew that it must lead to the rear of the house that he had seen as he approached the remote town earlier that day.

Iron Eyes tapped his spurs and steered the grey into the lane to search for the large building. The horse cantered as its rider stood in the stirrups and looked over the high fencing.

For more than 300 yards there

seemed to be nothing but trees neatly fenced off. Then he saw it.

Again Iron Eyes reined in hard. This time he drew the reins up to his chest. The horse stopped as the bounty hunter balanced and peered over the fence.

The house was well-illuminated.

At least forty men were milling in and around the substantial building as Fontaine waved his arms around conducting their every move.

Iron Eyes pulled his reins up and tied them to an overhead branch. He then leaned from his horse until his hands gripped the top of the fence. Ignoring the pain in his leg, he shook his left boot free of its stirrup and placed it on top of the saddle. He pushed until his thin body cleared the wooden obstacle.

Iron Eyes landed silently inside the fenced-off garden. He lay on his belly and spied on the almost frantic activity twenty yards ahead of him. The gunslingers were stripped to the waist. Their faces and torsos were being covered in some sort of coloured grease. Fontaine had a pile of ragged wigs and crude bandannas as well as a bag of long feathers. The men were indeed being made to look like Indians, Iron Eyes thought. Just as Ted Cooper had said.

None of the gunslingers would pass for any kind of Indian in daylight, but in the dark it was possible that they would fool the Easterner and his military escort.

Iron Eyes could not hear what Fontaine or his men were saying. He knew that he had to get closer if he were to overhear the details of the man's plans.

The bounty hunter looked all around him.

He saw that a handful of trees fringed the right-hand side of the yard. A few of the gunslingers were standing guard at various points. One was less than twenty feet away from him, leaning against a tree, sipping on a bottle of whiskey.

Iron Eyes wondered why Fontaine had to have any guards at all in his own back yard?

What did someone as powerful as Fontaine certainly was have to fear in this town? A town which he practically owned. Then it occurred to him.

Fontaine had only one man to fear in Hope.

He was that man!

Fontaine was afraid that Iron Eyes might spoil his play!

That had to be it!

The most powerful man in Hope was scared of Iron Eyes!

With his eyes still on the nearby guards, Iron Eyes rolled over and pulled both his guns from his belt. He pushed them down into his deep coat-pockets and then hauled out his long Bowie knife from his right boot neck. He placed the blade between his teeth and bit down upon it.

It tasted of rust and the blood of countless victims.

Then he started to crawl.

15

Iron Eyes moved silently. Like a snake, he seemed to slither along the dark edge of the large fenced-in yard, Even needle-sharp brambles could not slow his determined progress. The large trees had been there long before any men had found this remote place. Their stout trunks supported hefty branches and large leaves. This was all the cover the infamous bounty hunter required to reach his goal unseen. The nearby guard was between him and the men he wished to overhear.

The shadows which gave Iron Eyes protection also masked any clear view of the gunslinger whom Fontaine had placed on sentry duty.

Iron Eyes shifted his weight from one elbow to another as his long thin body reached the back of the tree upon which the guard was leaning.

The bounty hunter stopped and stared up from behind the tall lush grass that fringed the entire boundary of the extensive enclosed area. The smell of the whiskey that the armed guard was drinking from the bottle drifted down into the flared nostrils of Iron Eyes.

His bullet-coloured eyes studied the man as if he were a mere animal just about to be slaughtered. To Iron Eyes, every one of the men who accepted Fontaine's blood-money was less than vermin.

They deserved whatever fate he was about to dish out to them.

With the Bowie knife still firmly gripped in his teeth, Iron Eyes placed his hands on the trunk of the tree and slowly rose to his feet. Only the broad-girthed tree separated the two men. Iron Eyes did not require his knife for this kill, he drew it from his teeth and returned it to the neck of his boot.

When the bounty hunter had reached his full height he pressed his body against the bark and listened. He still had to get closer to Fontaine to hear what the man was saying. Only the sentry sipping on the whiskey bottle lay between himself and that goal.

All pain was forgotten.

Now he was the hunter again.

The hunter driven by a single thought, every sinew in his body tuned for one action: to kill the guard who stood between himself and the group of men close to the rear of the large house.

Iron Eyes took a step around the tree. He was closer now. A mere few feet from the shoulder of the man on sentry duty. The bounty hunter was close enough to strike.

He raised his hands.

The gunman returned the bottle to his lips. The hands of Iron Eyes struck out like a rattler. One hand went around the front of the man's throat as the other grabbed the bottle and pushed its neck into his mouth.

Then Iron Eyes hauled the gun-slinger off his feet and smashed him into the ground. Faster than the blink of an eye, the lean bounty hunter jumped on to the chest of his prey. He continued to hold the bottle and jerked it until its entire contents flowed into his victim's mouth.

Only when the clear-glass bottle was empty did Iron Eyes remove it from the mouth and cast it aside. He grabbed the throat of the choking man and glared down at him.

The gunslinger tried to pull the hand away.

He could not.

With not one ounce of mercy, Iron Eyes watched as his victim's eyeballs rolled up under the lids. He could feel the body shudder beneath him as it suffocated. Then the hands fell from the bony grip and landed limply on to the grass.

Iron Eyes knew when death had claimed another victim.

He got off the corpse, rose to his feet and stepped back to use the tree for cover. He stared across at the group of men who were now actually beginning to resemble Indians.

Iron Eyes dropped down and started to crawl again. This time he headed straight for Fontaine. He had covered half the distance between them when he began to understand the words that spewed from the well-liquored group.

'We gonna strike at night, boss?' Riley shouted out from behind a half-dozen half-naked men who were smothering each other with coloured grease. 'I thought that Injuns don't attack at night. Ain't that gonna be a mite suspicious?'

'Injuns ain't all superstitious, Riley!' Fontaine boomed.

'We gonna wait for them to head out from Apache Wells or are we attacking the way station itself?' Keno queried.

Fontaine removed his own fancy shirt and dipped his hands into the tub of coloured grease. He started to cover his own face and body with the vile concoction.

'It'd be a lot easier if we could wait

until they headed out from the way station, boys,' he answered. 'Trouble is, they won't leave there until after sunrise. I reckon they'd cotton on to us not being Indians damn fast in the light of day. No, we have to attack at night!'

'Mighty risky!' Keno was quick to note. 'That place is like a small fort! It can be defended!'

Fontaine laughed.

'It sure can be defended if the folks there know they're gonna be attacked, Keno. But them folks ain't got that kind of information, have they? We'll be able to ride straight in through their gates and start slaughtering before they have any idea what's happening! Right?'

Iron Eyes heard the unanimous roar of approval. The gunslingers were in a frenzied mood. A killing mood, fuelled by hard liquor and money.

The bounty hunter had heard enough.

Ted Cooper had been right.

Now all Iron Eyes had to do was get out of this place and ride to warn the soldiers and Carmichael at Apache Wells.

It was not quite as straightforward as it sounded.

He turned and started to crawl across the ground back to where he had left the dead body between the trees. He was almost there when his keen instincts heard something. He stopped and turned his head. He stared through his long limp hair and saw another of the guards. He was walking beside the fence towards the very spot where Iron Eyes had left the body.

Iron Eyes glanced behind him.

Fontaine and the others were still laughing, totally unaware of anything apart from the task of making themselves look like Indians. The bounty hunter pushed himself up off the ground. He ran low and fast. The guard had just cleared the second of the trees when Iron Eyes hit hard and high.

The impact winded the gunfighter.

They both fell.

They wrestled furiously in the ditch

beside the fence. Fists flew in both directions until the bounty hunter managed to force his adversary down. Iron Eyes balanced with one hand over the mouth of the startled guard as fingers clawed at his face.

Then Iron Eyes felt the gunman reach down for one of his holstered guns. Iron Eyes raised a knee and pressed it down on the man's gun hand. Without any hesitation the bounty hunter grabbed the knife from his teeth and went to ram it into the man's chest. The gunslinger used his left hand to grab Iron Eyes' wrist.

Both men glared at one another.

It was now a battle of willpower as well as strength.

The Bowie knife hovered above the chest of Fontaine's henchman as Iron Eyes strained to force it down. He knew that he dare not allow this man to call out and alert the others. The arms of both men shook violently. The tip of the blade touched the guard's shirt, then it was forced up again. Then Iron Eyes felt the powerful knee of his opponent hit him in the middle of his back.

He rocked but retained his position.

The man kneed him once more. Pain ripped through every muscle in the lean body but Iron Eyes would not allow any weakness to show in his scarred features.

Iron Eyes head-butted the man beneath him. He could tell that his foe was dazed.

Then he decided to outwit the man. If he could not force the blade down into his opponent, he would do the opposite. Iron Eyes pulled his knife hand up and out of the grip of the guard. Then a punch caught his chin as the frantic man fought for his life.

The bounty hunter could taste the blood in his mouth. He spat it into the eyes of his prey. As the man's left hand went towards his eyes to wipe away the bloody spittle Iron Eyes stabbed the long blade into the chest of the temporarily blinded guard. He felt it go right through the chest.

He dragged it out and then repeated the action a dozen times more. He only stopped when he was certain that the guard was as dead as his companion a few yards away. He pulled the Bowie knife out of the bloody chest and wiped its blade on the dead man's sleeve.

The fight had exhausted him. Sweat poured from his scalp and traced down along the ancient scars. His cold narrowed eyes watched as it dripped from the ends of the strands of limp hair on to the body between his kneeling legs. He pushed his long fingers through the wet wisps and looked back at the men who seemed to be rejoicing wildly. Iron Eyes wondered whether they might not be celebrating a little prematurely.

Iron Eyes forced himself up on to his feet. He pushed the knife down into the neck of his boot and leaned against the nearest tree.

His chest heaved as his pitifully thin body tried to suck in enough air to fill his lungs. His eyes narrowed as he studied the branches of the trees, which formed a canopy and reached far over the wall of fencing.

Iron Eyes reached up and grabbed at the nearest branch. He pulled his lightweight body up off the ground and into the dense broad-leafed refuge.

He carefully steadied himself on the widest of one of the tree's branches. One that went out over the fence.

Iron Eyes spread his arms wide and walked out along the branch, using those that were higher to maintain his balance. When he could see the ground of the narrow lane below him he sat down and dangled his long legs in mid-air. Iron Eyes lowered himself until he was hanging only a few feet above the dusty ground of the dark lane.

For what seemed like an eternity he just hung by his bony hands and looked down at the ground below his feet. Thoughts of the savage leg-wound filled his thoughts. Iron Eyes knew that if he were to land badly and it were to start bleeding again, it would be doubtful whether he would have time to stanch its bleeding a second time.

Mustering every ounce of his dogged determination, he released his grip and dropped to the ground. The bounty hunter steadied himself, then glanced down at his torn pants' leg and the gruesome wound it revealed. The cauterized flesh was inflamed from the brutal fight he had just survived, yet the skin was still somehow intact.

With the raised voices of Fontaine and his cohorts still ringing in his ears, he headed straight towards his grey horse.

Ignoring the pain which racked his entire body, Iron Eyes grabbed the saddle horn and threw himself on to his saddle. He poked both boots into his stirrups and tugged the reins until they came free of the overhead branch.

He dragged the neck of the horse to his right.

Iron Eyes spurred.

16

The land beyond the fertile range was little more than countless miles of dry sand and desert vegetation. Even a black moonless sky could not slow the progress of the solitary rider who rode beneath its magnificent canopy. The dim eerie light cast an awe-inspiring atmosphere across the flat plain. But the lone horseman did not notice that. All he could think about was reaching his destination before Fontaine and his band of deadly killers.

As was his way, Iron Eyes did not show the horse beneath him any mercy. He spurred, cursed and whipped the animal and forced it to continue galloping far beyond its own endurance. He had only one thought in his mind. He had to reach the way station at Apache Wells and warn Carmichael and his military escort of the impending attack by Fontaine and his hired guns.

There was no sense of duty in the bounty hunter as his mount continued to obey his new master's brutal will.

Iron Eyes was driven by only one motive.

He wanted the reward money he was owed and knew that if anyone could get it for him, it was the man he sought.

The hoofs of the grey raced across the sandy terrain beneath the black star-filled sky.

As with all the horses that had the misfortune to find themselves being ridden by the bounty hunter, its flesh was covered in blood as the spurs continued to be thrust into it.

Iron Eyes stood in his stirrups as the horse thundered across the desert. He could see the distant light of flickering torches against the black sky.

He had spotted the way station.

There was no more pain now. Iron Eyes felt nothing as he drove the exhausted animal beneath him directly towards the distant torchlights which lured him towards them.

Apache Wells was more than just another way station. It had once been a trading post when the land was filled with hunters, trappers and Indians. Built of adobe bricks which, at the base, were over six feet wide and covered in three additional inches of mud, mud which had been baked harder than cement in the blazing Western sun. The high walls which surrounded the buildings, stables and corrals had parapets designed to enable those inside to repel any attack from outside. Two large gates set at either end of the long courtyard enabled entry and exit of stagecoaches without their being required to turn around in the restricted space between the buildings.

Yet for all its defensive features, it appeared to the rider who approached to be deserted.

Iron Eyes' keen vision soon noted that there were no men guarding the way station's high walls. He galloped closer. The gates were wide open.

The bounty hunter drove on furiously towards his goal. He only slowed when he reached the sturdy adobe walls. Iron Eyes reined back and held the lathered-up mount in check.

He stared through the open gates.

It was quiet. Too damn quiet.

There should be at least twenty men inside the way station, Iron Eyes thought to himself. Could they all be asleep? The question lingered in the mind of the grim-faced rider. That seemed impossible. Had the men who ran this remote fortress become so complacent that they no longer took even the most basic of precautions?

He found it difficult to comprehend. In a land full of badmen and the scum that had been driven from more civilized states, it just seemed inexplicable to the bounty hunter.

Iron Eyes gripped his reins tightly and stared around the courtyard as his horse moved nervously beneath his saddle. Could his suspicions be correct?

Was the way station deserted? He knew that there was only one way to discover the truth. He had to venture inside the walled stagecoach depot.

His eyes glanced up at the wooden board that spanned the distance between the walls to each side of the gates. Even in the starlight he could still read the name.

Apache Wells.

At least he knew that he had managed to find the place that he had sought for so many gruelling hours of riding across the dry sandy terrain.

But why were there no people to be seen?

There were lanterns lit along the two buildings that stood a hundred yards away beside a corral and stables. People must have lit the lanterns at sundown, he thought.

Iron Eyes tapped his spurs and urged the grey into the long yard. The mount had just cleared the doors when Iron Eyes heard something.

It was the sound of humming.

He rose in his stirrups and dragged a gun from one of his deep pockets. Then he felt the rope encircle his chest. Before he could claw back on the gun's hammer the rope tightened.

Iron Eyes felt himself being dragged over the cantle of his saddle. He slid over the hind quarters of the grey before falling.

He hit the ground hard.

As his eyes opened he saw the starlight trace along the barrels of rifles as men came down the ladders from the parapets.

Every barrel was aimed straight at him.

17

The half-dozen troopers had done a good job on their unsuspecting prisoner. They had used the stocks of their Springfield rifles to knock any resistance from the bounty hunter, even though he had been winded and helpless after hitting the hard ground when hauled off his saddle. The troopers had tightened the rope around Iron Eyes until he could hardly breathe. It ensured that he remained helpless as they beat him mercilessly. Blood flowed from a deep gash above his left eye where the imprint of a boot could still be plainly seen in the lantern-light. Only after satisfying their basic instincts did the troopers decide to drag their dazed trophy into the way station's main building.

They threw Iron Eyes to the floor.

Roped like a maverick at branding

time, the bounty hunter lay on his side and stared at the men who paraded triumphantly around him. There were war drums ringing inside his head, which almost blotted out the laughter that came from the mouths of his captors. Almost but not quite.

He wanted to kill them all!

Given half a chance, he would have!

Few creatures managed to arouse the venom of the bounty hunter quite as much as cavalrymen. Iron Eyes had encountered thousands of them over the years, and they all seemed to be cast from the same mould. None could equal the basic integrity of the average Apache. Iron Eyes hated most Indians, especially Apaches, but they were still better than troopers in his judgement. Most enlisted men were little more than mindless trash. They were soldiers because they could do nothing else. Without orders, most of them reverted to being little better than animals in his estimation.

Even as blood dripped into his eyes

from the gash on his temple, Iron Eyes saw a door open to his left. His eyes darted to it and viewed the overweight Herbert Carmichael as he entered in his long nightshirt. Even dazed, Iron Eyes could not take his eyes off the beautiful Florence, who was almost hidden by her father's immense bulk as he walked towards him.

'What have we here?' Carmichael asked as he looked down on the troopers' roped prisoner.

Captain Bob Sherwood walked from the opposite side of the room across the floorboards. He brought his highly polished boots to a halt a few inches away from the face of Iron Eyes.

'Who is this creature, Captain?' Carmichael continued.

'I'm not sure, sir,' Sherwood replied. He looked across the man on the floor to his sentries. 'What is this, Sergeant? Where did it come from?'

'Injun! We seen this critter heading here, Captain,' the burly sergeant said. 'He was headed from across the plain.

We let him ride in and then roped him. Yep, he's an Injun all right! Looks like an Apache to me.'

A furious Iron Eyes forced himself up until he was in a kneeling position. He looked through the strands of bloody hair at the officer and raged.

'Apache? I ain't no damn Apache!' he snarled. 'I hates Apaches! I hates all Injuns!'

Sherwood leaned over and looked straight into the gruesome features of the hogtied man. He smiled, then taunted the bounty hunter.

'If ya ain't an Apache, what are ya?'

'They call me Iron Eyes!' the kneeling man growled. 'I'm a bounty hunter and I came here to warn ya that this place is gonna be attacked by a bunch of badmen dressed up as redskins! Damned if I know why I bothered now after the reception committee ya gave me!'

Sherwood straightened up. 'Badmen dressed up as redskins? Is that so? I think that my men might have bin a little rough with ya. Ya brains bin kicked loose by the sound of it, Iron Eyes!'

A ripple of amused laughter went around the room.

'And who are these badmen you mentioned, Iron Eyes?' Carmichael asked wryly.

Iron Eyes looked up at the territorial secretary governor. His icy stare stopped the man from laughing.

'A critter named Fontaine! Brewster Fontaine! He owns this territory and he don't want the likes of you bringing no civilization here! He got himself a whole bunch of outlaws on his payroll and they're disguising themselves as red-skins to come here and wipe most of ya out. He intends leaving a few of ya alive to tell them folks back East that this place is just too dangerous to even consider turning into a state!'

Herbert Carmichael looked at the captain. His expression was grim. He cleared his throat loudly.

'Fontaine! That's the name of the man that I'm meant to meet up with,

Sherwood! Brewster Fontaine! He is meant to help me arrange an election in these parts!'

Sherwood pointed at his troopers.

'Pick this man up!'

They did.

Iron Eyes stood and glanced at the men who surrounded him with a hatred he could not hide. He looked at the young female standing behind her broad-shouldered father. She seemed out of place here, he thought. This was no land for such an innocent.

'Any chance of ya gettin' this rope off me, Captain?' he asked. 'I'd like to suck some air into my lungs!'

Sherwood nodded and pointed to his men.

'Release him!' he commanded. 'Give him back whatever weaponry you relieved him of!'

Again the troopers obeyed.

Iron Eyes felt the rope slacken and fall to his feet. He rubbed his forearms in an attempt to get the blood flowing back into his long thin arms. He accepted the matched pair of Navy Colts from one of the troopers. The thought of killing all the men in blue flashed through his mind for a brief moment. He then dropped the guns into the deep pockets of his coat.

'I still reckon he's a filthy Injun, Captain!' the sergeant said gruffly.

Iron Eyes turned and looked straight into the faces of the troopers. He concentrated on the man with the stripes on his shirt-sleeves.

'Injun?' he snarled.

The sergeant went to speak again. He did not manage it. The bounty hunter's bony knuckles caught him on the end of his whiskered chin. There was a cracking noise as teeth shattered. The trooper staggered and then fell heavily on to his back. He nursed his jaw for a few moments before rolling over and crawling to the nearest spittoon. He knelt beside it and spat blood and broken fragments of teeth into the brass vessel.

Sherwood inhaled.

'I could have you arrested for that!' he told Iron Eyes.

'And I could kill the whole bunch of ya faster than ya can blink!' the bounty hunter boasted. 'But it ain't my way! I don't waste bullets on folks that ain't got bounty on their heads!'

'Steady, men!' Carmichael urged. 'Let's not fight amongst ourselves!'

Again Iron Eyes looked at the frightened female. He lowered his fists and nodded.

'Why did you come here, Iron Eyes?' Sherwood asked. 'What is ya motive to warn us? Ya don't seem the sort to give a damn about anyone except yaself!'

'Money!' Iron Eyes snarled as he touched the bleeding cut above his eye. 'Bounty money! I'm owed and I want payin'! Figured that if I warned ya all, ya might make sure I get my bounty!'

Carmichael nodded.

'I see that you are a man who speaks his mind! You cut straight to the chase! I like that!'

Iron Eyes wiped the blood off his

fingers on to his shirt-front.

'I killed over twenty of them outlaws that works for Fontaine 'coz they tried to kill me! Trouble is he owns the bank in Hope and wouldn't pay me!'

Carmichael chuckled.

'I can see his point! It must be upsetting having to pay someone for killing one's own employees!'

'Ya gonna make sure I gets my bounty or not?' Iron Eyes snapped. 'Make up ya mind, we ain't got much time!'

Carmichael shrugged.

'I shall, if you remain here and help us fight off this attack. Should it actually happen, that is!'

'Ya doubtin' my word, Carmichael?' the bounty hunter stepped closer to the large man. 'Ya think I'm lyin'?'

'Are you willing to stay here and fight with us?' Sherwood repeated the question.

Iron Eyes looked at the silent female again. She was terrified by his appearance. He had seen that look so many times before that he had grown used to it. He sighed and then looked back to the army captain.

'I'll stick around!' Iron Eyes said. 'I'll make sure that nothin' happens to that little lady!'

'What do you mean, sir?' Carmichael pushed his daughter behind him.

'I mean that you boys can fend for yaselves, but that girl can't! Fontaine's critters will have to kill me to get to her! Savvy?'

The secretary governor nodded.

'I think so!'

'Good!'

'When do you think these outlaws will attack?'

Iron Eyes looked at the men who surrounded him and raised his voice so that none of them could misunderstand his words.

'Listen up! We ain't got much time! Fontaine can't be far behind me! That means he has maybe forty or more gunmen headed straight down our throats! We have to secure this place so that they can't just ride in! Get the way station crew out of their beds and arm them! We have to man them walls and start shootin' as soon as they gets into range!'

'I give the orders here, Iron Eyes!' Sherwood said waving his finger at the bounty hunter.

Iron Eyes stepped toe to toe with the cavalry officer and looked him in the eye.

'Not any more, Captain!' he argued. 'Not any more!'

18

Only the light of a million stars suspended from a black sky had guided the formidable collection of riders to within a mere mile of Apache Wells. The forty-one horsemen had thundered across the arid wastelands towards the distant fiery beacons. Drawn like moths to a naked flame, the lethal army of killers had made good time. Fuelled by hard liquor and the promise of rewards beyond their wildest dreams, they had followed their leader like a pack of ravenous wolves seeking out fresh prey.

Just like Iron Eyes before them, they had spotted the torches on the way station's high walls long before they had actually been able to make out its adobe walls bathed in starlight.

Like a warlord of ancient times, Brewster Fontaine had led his men from the front for the entire journey. It was something which he had never done before, but he had never faced the possibility of having his entire fortune stripped from him before either.

He was in no mood to sit back and wait for his henchmen to do his bidding this time. This was one occasion on which he had to ensure that the job was done exactly right.

There was no room for error.

A kingdom was at stake. Fontaine had worked long and hard to take control of the vast untamed territory. It had taken genius to outwit an entire population until they were little more than his slaves.

Now it was at risk from faceless men back East. If not stopped, they would not only steal the land he controlled, but his fortune would also be at risk. He had heard of what had happened to other men such as himself when territories suddenly became states. Men who were richer than royalty one day were penniless the next. Fontaine had vowed that that fate would never overtake him.

He would die fighting to retain his riches and power. No Easterner would rob him of all the things he had managed to acquire over the years.

Fontaine sat astride his horse and stared at the distant adobe fortress. He knew that the only way that he could be certain that his hired gunmen did exactly as he had ordered was to lead them himself.

It had been a long time since he had killed anything, but he had not forgotten how. The lust for blood still remained in his bitter, twisted soul.

Fontaine cast his eyes to either side of him as he urged his mount on. He was satisfied with the transformation of his henchmen. The half-light gave the disguised riders the appearance of actually being an Indian war party. He had even purchased forty-one blankets to hide their saddles from any keen-eyed trooper who might survive the attack.

Any uneducated eye that happened

upon his attacking force would see only Indians. Greased skin and body-paint created the illusion. Yet they all knew that they would have to complete their task well before the sun rose again. None of them would ever pass for being a genuine Apache in the light of day. Dawn was their enemy as much as those who rested inside the way station.

The horses thundered onward toward Apache Wells.

Unlike the bounty hunter who had preceded them, they had not driven their mounts to exhaustion. These men had stopped to water their horses twice on the long journey from Hope.

Reaching a ridge, Fontaine hauled rein. Dust swept up towards the stars as the horse dug its hoofs into the sand. The forty horsemen stopped their own mounts beside their boss. For a few moments the way station was masked by the dust clouds that rolled over the terrain before them.

Only when it had settled did they see Apache Wells clearly.

Keno moved his horse closer to the silent Fontaine.

'I told ya that the place was like a fort!' he said, pointing at the moonlit adobe structure a mile ahead. 'Look at it! The folks who built that thing did it to stop critters like us attacking them!'

'Quiet, ya fool!' Fontaine muttered thoughtfully.

Riley adjusted the crude wig he had been forced to wear and looked across at Fontaine.

'Do ya really reckon we can get the better of them bastards, boss?' he asked.

'I'd say that they're all asleep in their beds, Frank,' the confident Fontaine replied. 'There ain't bin any Indians in these parts for years. That breeds a false sense of security. I think we can just ride in and kill them all.'

'I sure hope so!' Keno shrugged.

'The last time I came this way they didn't even close the gates at night, boys!' Fontaine smiled. 'They just left them wide open! Yep, wide open like a two-dollar whore's legs!'

'Ya bin here before, boss?' Keno asked.

'Damn right!' Fontaine said. 'I know the inside of that place like the back of my hand! I know the lay-out of every room in the main building!'

Suddenly the confidence of their leader filled the rest of the horsemen with inspiration. They seemed excited again.

'We gonna kill all them soldier blues, boss?' Walt Jason piped up.

Fontaine turned and looked at the young gunslinger. Even the coloured grease which was smothered over his features could not hide the smile that went from ear to ear.

'Yep! Every one of them!'

'Then who we gonna let live?' Riley queried.

'The coach-driver!' Fontaine answered. 'He's a civilian. He'll make a darn good witness.'

'What about the station workers?'

Jason wondered aloud.

'We only kill them if they gets in the way!' Fontaine said coldly. 'They'll make good witnesses! Reckon they'll tell folks about the Injun war party that attacked and massacred the big man from back East and his cavalry bodyguards!'

'What about this Carmichael critter?' Keno wondered as he fought the effects of the whiskey which fogged his brain. 'Do we kill him?'

'Damn right we do!' Fontaine laughed. 'He dies like the soldiers! He's our main target! We kill him and I doubt if they'll ever be able to find anyone back East dumb enough to volunteer to replace him!'

The horsemen were laughing as Fontaine produced two bottles of hard liquor from the bags secreted beneath the blanket that hid his saddle from prying eyes. There were still two more bottles of whiskey remaining in the satchels. They were for later when their deed had been done.

He tossed one to Jason and the other to Riley.

'Take a mouthful of whiskey each and pass the bottles along, boys!' Fontaine ordered. 'This is a job that'll be easier with fire in ya bellies!'

'Will this stop them damn Easterners comin' here to steal our land, boss?' Riley asked.

'It might slow them up a tad!' Fontaine smiled. 'Make them think twice about tryin' to push their yella-belly laws down our throats!'

By the time the two bottles had been passed along the line of riders and reached the last of Fontaine's henchmen they were empty.

Fontaine gathered up his reins. His eyes burned out across the distance between the starlit fortress and his line of primed riders.

'C'mon, boys! We got us some scalpin' to do!'

The shrewd businessman knew exactly how to get his men to do his bidding. All it took was the promise of enough money and just the correct amount of whiskey.

With Fontaine at their head, the troop of murderous riders thundered on towards the fiery torches perched upon the high walls of the way station. No genuine band of Apaches could have equalled the blood-chilling sight.

★   ★   ★

The stagecoach company workers had just secured the two gates set at opposite ends of the way station's long courtyard when Iron Eyes shouted out to the rest of the well-armed men perched all around the high parapets.

'Here they come!' the bounty hunter yelled as he stared over the top of the wall at the unmistakable sight of horsemen headed straight towards them. 'Cock ya rifles!'

The sound of Springfield rifles being readied for action echoed around the high parapets. The bounty hunter marched along the wall and checked the kneeling soldiers as they trained their weapons on the large band of horsemen.

'Remember, boys,' Iron Eyes growled, 'ya gotta kill as many of them as ya can! If'n they gets in here, they'll surely slaughter us for sure!'

Captain Sherwood raced across the courtyard from the main building and clambered up one of the ladders. He reached Iron Eyes' side and stared out into the starlit wasteland which stretched before him.

A cold chill traced up his spine.

'Dear Lord! You were tellin' the truth! There are at least forty of the bastards headed here, and they're disguised as redskins!'

'And they figure on killin' most of us if'n they gets half a chance, Captain!' Iron Eyes added. He drew one of his Navy Colts from his deep coat-pocket and cocked its hammer until it fully locked. 'Fontaine ain't in the mood for no talkin'! He's gonna kill most of us if he can!'

Sherwood looked along the parapets and yelled at the top of his voice at his troopers.

'Start shootin' when they get into range, men! That's an order! We ain't takin' any prisoners!'

Iron Eyes glanced at the obviously nervous officer who stood beside him, shaking.

'Now ya talkin' my kinda lingo, Sherwood!' he muttered.

The army captain produced a pair of field binoculars from a small bag attached to his belt. He raised them to his eyes and adjusted the focus.

'Great heavens. They are whitemen, Iron Eyes!' He lowered the binoculars in shock. 'I thought that ya had to be wrong! I just couldn't believe that whitemen would stoop so low!'

'Yep, they're white, OK, and they're loaded for bear!' Iron Eyes assured him. 'Look at all them rifles and six-shooters glinting like gold pieces! Just like I told ya!'

'I apologize for doubtin' ya, Iron

Eyes!' A bead of sweat appeared from the band of the captain's black hat. It trailed down the side of the officer's face. The bounty hunter stared at the man who, for his part, could not take his eyes from the approaching horsemen. 'I know little of this devilish land or the vermin who occupy it!'

'Ya ever seen action before, Sherwood?' Iron Eyes asked. He watched the expression on the officer's face.

'Nothin' to match this!' came the honest reply. 'What'll we do? What should I do?'

Iron Eyes placed a cigar between his teeth, struck a match and lit it. He inhaled the acrid smoke and allowed it to linger in his lungs for a while before speaking in a low tone that only the captain could hear.

'Just follow my lead, Sherwood! I'm just gonna try and kill them all! Copy that and ya ain't gonna go far wrong!'

Before the shaking cavalry officer could speak again, the air around them rang out as deafening bullets rained in on them.

Instinctively, Iron Eyes placed a hand on Sherwood's shoulder and pushed the man down violently so that the captain was below the parapet's solid adobe wall. Chunks of the wall exploded as dozens of bullets sought out their targets. Yet the bounty hunter did not flinch as he sucked on the smoke and stared out at the approaching riders.

'Open up on them, boys!' Iron Eyes ordered the troopers. As one the kneeling soldiers started to fire.

'Why don't you get down, Iron Eyes?' Sherwood shouted as dust showered over him from bullets tearing into the top of the wall. 'Take cover, man!'

Iron Eyes did not duck down himself. He turned his painfully thin body sideways on to the approaching riders and then raised his Navy Colt until it was at arm's length. He focused on the gun's sights and then started to fire. The speed of his thumb as it clawed the hammer back after each shot stunned the kneeling Sherwood. He had never seen anyone who could fire as fast as this man.

What he could not see was that every one of the shots hit the riders. Three of the gunslingers were knocked off their horses before Iron Eyes had fired the last of his six shots.

Only when he needed to reload did the bounty hunter crouch down beside Sherwood.

'Where did ya learn to shoot like that, Iron Eyes?'

'It comes natural when ya don't like many folks, Captain,' the bounty hunter answered honestly. 'In my profession ya gotta hit what ya aims at the first time. Ya might not get a second chance, ya know?'

'But why didn't ya take cover sooner?'

The bounty hunter shook the brass casings from the gun and started to push fresh bullets into its smoking chambers.

'Ya ever tried shootin' from a galloping horse? Ain't easy hittin' anythin'!' Iron Eyes closed the Navy Colt and cocked its hammer again. 'I figured I had me some time before they could judge the distance with them Winchesters!'

Even above the sound of the soldiers' rifle fire, both of the kneeling men could hear the riders pass below them as Fontaine led his gang to the nearest of the locked gates, then round the walls to the other.

Fontaine had taken casualties and did not like it. The first of the tall gates were locked and the walls were manned with a score or more rifles. He drove his horse on. He stayed close to the wall and headed round to the other gate. Five of his henchmen trailed him as others were knocked from their horses by the cavalry's lead. Frank Riley whipped his horse and drew level with his boss. A massive hole in his left shoulder spat blood over Fontaine.

'They've suckered us in to a turkey-shoot, boss!' Riley shouted out. 'How'd they know we was comin'?'

'Who cares? Just stick with me, Frank,' Fontaine ordered. 'I got me a plan to stick the fox in this hen-house!'

The half-dozen riders drove along the base of the sturdy wall. They had left Keno and the main body of horsemen shooting it out with the soldiers gathered near to Iron Eyes and the army captain. Fontaine had another goal and another way to gain entrance into the Apache Wells fortress.

Fontaine stopped his lathered-up mount beneath the big gates and pointed his rifle up at the cavalry men. Within a mere blink of an eye, he and his cohorts had opened up with deadly volleys of bullets. Soldiers cascaded off the walls and landed heavily in a row before the disguised riders. Fontaine pushed a cigar between his dry lips and lit it quickly. He sucked on it until its tip glowed like the tail of a firefly.

'Cover me, boys!' Fontaine commanded his henchmen.

They did.

Fontaine leapt to the ground and pulled the blanket off his saddle. He opened the leather flaps of the bags which were tied to the cantle of his saddle and removed one of the bottles of whiskey. He threw it with all his force at the dry gates.

The bottle shattered into a million slivers, spewing its contents all over the weathered wood and surrounding brush.

'What ya doin', boss?' Riley yelled out as he continued to fire his Winchester at the soldiers above them.

'You'll see!' Fontaine shouted back to his top gun.

The riders watched as their leader removed the cigar from his mouth, blew on the glowing tip and then tossed it at the alcohol-splashed wooden gates.

The combination of tinder-dry wood, hard rotgut liquor and brush was a volatile mixture. When the burning tobacco was added, the flames erupted like a volcano. Within a mere few seconds the entire gate was engulfed in flames. Then Fontaine threw the last bottle at the blazing wall before him. Flames rose thirty feet into the air.

From the opposite end of the way station Iron Eyes prepared to start shooting down at Keno and the main body of gunslingers.

'As soon as them riders comes below ya, shoot as many of the swine as ya can, boys!' the bounty hunter shouted out to the troopers who manned the opposite wall.

Suddenly one of the station workers screamed out.

'Fire! Fire!'

Every one of the men perched on the parapets looked at the elderly station worker and then to what he was frantically pointing at. Every one of the men on the high walkways stood in horror and disbelief.

Iron Eyes gritted his teeth and growled.

'Get ready, Sherwood! We got less

than a minute or so before that gate falls and Fontaine and his cronies ride in!' he snapped, making his way to the nearest ladder. He started to climb down to the floor of the way station. 'I'm gonna go protect Carmichael and the girl!'

Flames had already risen over the surface of the gates and were eating through the old wooden boards so quickly that they were already starting to crumble in blackened chunks.

As Iron Eyes raced across the courtyard, bathed in the light of the fire, towards the main building, he thought about Brewster Fontaine.

He had underestimated the man!

Fontaine was far more dangerous than he had given him credit for. As the bounty hunter reached the building he wondered whether that error of judgement might prove fatal.

Iron Eyes shouldered the door open and glanced around the large room. The stalwart figure of Herbert Carmichael and his terrified daughter were highlighted by crimson shafts of flickering light which cut in through the gaps between the window shutters.

'Quick! If ya wanna live, follow me!' The bounty hunter waved the barrel of his Colt at them before he made his way towards the corridor which led to the dozen or more guest-rooms on the ground floor. With every step Iron Eyes studied the rest of the building's interior. A wooden staircase led up to a landing and a solitary door. The tall thin figure continued towards the corridor, which was bathed in shadow.

'What's happening out there, Iron Eyes?' Carmichael asked breathlessly.

'Move fast!' Iron Eyes ordered bluntly.

They did.

The bounty hunter found the only room that did not have a window and then ushered them into it.

'What's happening, Iron Eyes?' Carmichael repeated his question. 'I thought you said that we were safe with the station gates locked!'

'I did!' Iron Eyes' bony hands pushed both confused people inside the small room.

'Has something changed?'

The grim-faced bounty hunter was about to reply when he caught sight of the woman's face. He decided not to answer the question for fear of frightening the young Florence even more. There was something about her which intrigued him. She was so fragile, yet more beautiful than any other he had ever set eyes upon.

'Barricade yaselves in here!' he ordered. 'Use the chairs and bed to stop them bustin' the door down. Hide in the corner in case them varmints shoot through it! This door is the only way in or out of this room! OK?'

The young woman nodded as her father spoke once more.

'Do you think we'll survive this, Iron Eyes?'

Again Iron Eyes glanced at the timid Florence, who clung to her father's arm. There was no supposing that she was strong enough to hear the truth, he thought. He decided to try and give her a scrap of hope to cling to.

'Yep! They'll not get ya!' he said. He pulled the door shut and listened as its bolt was slid across. He paused until he heard the furniture in the room being moved to behind the door before moving back into the centre of the large room.

Suddenly the sound of something landing on the roof above his head stopped the bounty hunter in his tracks. Dust filtered down over him. He raised his gun and listened as the noise tracked across the wooden shingles.

His keen ears listened until he saw the body of one of the troopers who had been manning the parapet behind him fall limply to the ground in front of the open doorway.

Iron Eyes rushed to the crumpled body, leaned over and touched the blood-soaked neck. There was no sign of any pulse. Iron Eyes looked at the gruesome bullet wound in the side of the trooper's skull. He then rose up to his full height. His gaze darted around the parapets. At least half the troopers were either dead or wounded.

Captain Sherwood was still battling alongside his men as they continued to fire their single-shot rifles down at Fontaine's riders outside the walls.

Iron Eyes glanced to his right. It had only been a matter of minutes since the gates had been drowned in an ocean of flames, yet they were already disintegrating. Sparks floated on the warm night air and landed on the shingle rooftops of the way station buildings. The fire had already spread to the tinder-dry stables.

Scores of terrified horses trapped within whinnied as they struggled to escape the smoke and fire which now was taking hold in the rafters and walls.

Iron Eyes was about to move to the closest trough and attempt to douse the flames with water when he heard a strange cracking sound. He spun on his heels and stared at the flaming gates. Even thirty feet away from the inferno, he could feel the incredible heat burning his scarred features. He dropped his gun into his deep pocket, grabbed a bucket and dipped it into the trough. Then he saw one half of the gate buckle on its hinges and fall. A cloud of smoke and red-hot cinders erupted and drifted into the heart of the courtyard.

'This ain't good!' he told himself.

Fontaine and his men did not wait for the fire to consume the gates entirely before they ducked and drove their mounts through the pile of burning embers. A million fiery splinters sent a tidal wave of smouldering sparks across the courtyard and up into the black sky as the riders finally breached the way station's defences.

The horsemen charged. Fontaine led what was left of his henchmen. Blinded by the ferocious flames and blistering heat, they all kept their heads low until they were certain they had ridden beyond the gates.

Iron Eyes watched as at least twenty riders rode straight at him. The bounty hunter could see the whites of the galloping horses' eyes as they pelted towards him.

Iron Eyes dropped the bucket and threw himself through the corral poles. He landed heavily as a few of the horses crashed into the fencing. Long poles were smashed from their uprights and crashed down over the bounty hunter. He scrambled away through the dust when the shooting started again.

Sherwood was getting his troopers to shoot down at their uninvited intruders from the parapets whilst Fontaine and his henchmen returned fire.

Gunsmoke mixed with the clouds of dust and black smoke that filled the entire courtyard.

Iron Eyes plucked one of his Navy Colts from his pocket and blasted at the nearest of the riders. He had fanned the gun's hammer six times, and watched as three of the riders fell from their mounts and landed in the dust. He dropped the gun into his coat-pocket again and staggered toward Carmichael's armoured coach. He dropped to the ground and crawled beneath it. The sound of bullets ricocheting off the coachwork rang in the bounty hunter's ears.

Then his attention was drawn back to the burning stables and the pitiful sound of the horses trapped inside it. Iron Eyes knew that stampeding horses in a confined space could cause a lot of trouble. If he managed to stay out of their way and the troopers remained up high on the walls, the only people who would be faced by that trouble were Fontaine and his ruthless riders.

The bounty hunter pushed himself up and raced to the stable doors. He lifted the pole which secured them off its metal cradles and cast it aside.

Iron Eyes was knocked off his feet as the doors were violently charged open by the alarmed animals. He blinked hard and then saw the horses stampeding out of the smoke-filled stables straight at him.

He rolled out of the way just in time. Countless hoofs pounded the ground and smashed into the heavily armoured coach, sending it over on to its side.

The horses continued onwards. Survival instinct guided the wide-eyed creatures now. They had to escape the choking smoke and deadly flames.

Iron Eyes watched the small herd gallop through the fence-poles and into the midst of the mounted riders. It was mayhem. Horsemen fell as their horses were knocked down. Screams filled the area as they were crushed under hoofs. Dust and smoke hid the sight of the carnage from the bounty hunter's keen eyes. But he could hear it all.

The sound of firing continued to ring out from all directions. It was the only thing which let him know that not all the horsemen within the way station were dead yet.

Fiery debris fell down from the stable's roof and landed all around the lean figure. Iron Eyes glanced up. He then realized that the fire was spreading far more quickly than he had thought possible. Now flames leapt the distance between the stable and the main building's roof which was now also alight.

Iron Eyes shook all the spent shells from his guns and reloaded swiftly. As he pushed the bullets into the empty chambers he tried to work out his next move.

Even through the dense dust he could see that some of the riders had managed to reach the front of the building where he had left Carmichael and Florence.

He knew he had to act fast.

Smoke and dust swirled around the area like a choking fog. It blinded him to the truth. The truth of how many of their attackers were still capable of killing.

Iron Eyes took three steps forward and caught a glimpse of the one man he recognized. Even though they were smothered in coloured grease, the features of Fontaine had been branded in the mind of the bounty hunter.

It was a face he could never forget.

Fontaine and a handful of his henchmen had thundered through the chaos and smoke beyond the fence-poles. They were still exchanging shots with the troopers outside the main building.

Iron Eyes leapt into action. He sped to where he had left Carmichael and his daughter. With every step he fired his guns through the dust and smoke at the riders.

He could not tell how many of his bullets had found their targets but it did not matter.

There was only one of the vicious horsemen that he really wanted to kill. The leader of the murderous riders was his only real prey. Iron Eyes knew that once Fontaine was dead, the rest of them would be like rattlers with their heads cut off.

He had to destroy Fontaine!

He also had to try and somehow get

Carmichael and his daughter out of the building which was now on fire!

Bullets suddenly stopped his advance as they tore through the air and shattered the wooden wall beside him. A million splinters showered over Iron Eyes. There was no way he could reach the front of the building. The gunmen were already there and they were fending off all attempts to dislodge them.

Iron Eyes could see Fontaine and the riders dismounting. They raced into the building, still shooting their rifles and handguns at the soldiers high above them.

The angry bounty hunter knew he would have to find another way into the building if he were to save Carmichael and Florence. He dropped both guns into his deep coat-pockets and then started to climb up the side wall of the large building. There was an open window on the wall, about twenty feet above the ground.

If he could get inside, that would

be the only way.

Flames were now dancing over a third of the tarred roof-shingles and molten fire dripped like rain over him. Yet even with the shoulders of his coat smouldering, Iron Eyes kept climbing.

With the dexterity of a desert lizard, Iron Eyes ascended the wall quickly. He reached the open window, dragged himself through it and dropped to the floor on the landing. Smoke was now billowing down from the rafters and filling the air with its choking stench. He raised himself up on to his feet again and screwed up his eyes.

It was almost impossible to see anything.

He carefully edged his way forward until he felt a wooden rail stop his progress.

The air was clearer down in the heart of the large room below him. He could see six of the heavily disguised men gathered around the door. They were firing their weaponry with a ferocity which had not abated even though they had lost so many of their cohorts.

The ceiling above his head started to blacken and then glow as the fire ate its way through the wood. A strange red light illuminated the high landing.

Silent, Iron Eyes remained above them. He reloaded his guns again from the loose bullets in his coat pockets. When both Navy Colts were ready he cocked their hammers.

'Fontaine!' he shouted out.

All six men turned and stared up at the awesome apparition.

Riley was still nursing the wound in his shoulder when he gasped:

'Iron Eyes!'

Fontaine jumped up with his Winchester in his hands. Smoke trailed from its hot barrel.

'What the hell is he doin' here?' he snarled as the rest of the men rose to their feet.

Iron Eyes had heard every word.

'I'm here to kill ya all!' he replied. 'Say ya prayers!'

'Kill him!' Fontaine screamed out. 'Kill the bastard!'

Every weapon was raised. Every trigger squeezed. A volley of bullets spewed from the barrels.

Like a defiant statue, Iron Eyes did not move an inch from the rail. As bullets tore past him he fired both his guns and watched as, one after another, the men fell dead around the raging Fontaine.

Only when Iron Eyes had destroyed each of the remaining hired guns did he train his guns on their leader and start down the wooden steps.

Fontaine felt the trigger of his rifle slacken as his index finger milked it. The rifle was empty.

He threw it to the floor.

'I'm unarmed, Iron Eyes! It's over! Ya can't shoot an unarmed man, can ya?'

Iron Eyes walked slowly toward him with no expression on his hideous face.

His unblinking eyes stared through the half-light at the sweating man.

He stopped ten feet from Fontaine. His thumbs pulled the gun hammers back again.

'I just recalled that ya got bounty on ya head, Fontaine! I seen ya poster back in Dodge a few years back. Dead or alive!'

'I give up! Ya got me! I don't know how, but ya won!' the sweating man stammered. 'Ya can't kill an unarmed man! Ya won! Don't ya understand? Ya won!'

'Not yet, I ain't,' Iron Eyes drawled slowly. Then he squeezed both his triggers. Two bullets tore through the man's guts. He watched as Fontaine was lifted off his feet and thrown through the open doorway. He crashed on to the boardwalk outside the building. 'Now I've won!'

Fire dripped down from the ceiling above the bounty hunter as he pushed both guns into his belt. He walked into the dark corridor to where he had left

Carmichael and the beautiful young woman.

He tapped the door with his bony knuckles.

'It's over!' he said.

Finale

Herbert Carmichael was true to his word. He ensured that Iron Eyes was paid every cent he was owed of the reward money on the heads of all the hired gunmen the bounty hunter had killed during the previous day. The territorial secretary had used some of the thousands of golden fifty-dollar pieces which were in Brewster Fontaine's own bank vault to pay Iron Eyes shortly after the diminished band of troopers and the armoured coach had eventually arrived at the town of Hope with their skeletal saviour.

They were a welcome sight to the residents of the remote settlement and confirmation that after so many years, they were rid of the deadly men who had ruled over them.

Captain Bob Sherwood could hardly believe that he had lost so many of his troopers in such a short period of time. Only eight of his men had survived unscathed. The rest were tied over their cavalry saddles, waiting for the undertaker to lay them to rest.

The cavalry officer could also not fathom how the long-haired bounty hunter somehow managed to get the better of so many lethal foes. He had learned a lot when he had been at West Point, but it paled into insignificance compared with what he had been taught by Iron Eyes.

Sherwood walked from his battered and bruised men to the bank as Carmichael and his daughter watched Iron Eyes place two swollen canvas sacks in each of his saddle-bag satchels on the back of his grey mount.

'That's a tidy sum you earned there, Iron Eyes!' he said as the bounty hunter stepped into his stirrup and hoisted himself up on to his saddle. 'But you certainly earned every penny of it! I cannot express my gratitude enough for the way you looked after my dear

Florence and myself. Thank you, Iron Eyes!'

Iron Eyes looked through his limp wisps of hair down at the two people as Sherwood joined them. He nodded silently and gave the beautiful woman a last look.

'Thank you, Iron Eyes!' Florence somehow managed to say. 'I shall never forget you.'

Iron Eyes gathered up his reins and turned the horse away from the hitching rail.

'I ain't gonna forget you either, ma'am!' he said.

'Where ya headed, Iron Eyes?' Sherwood asked as the grey walked towards him.

'Ain't figured that out yet, Captain,' the bounty hunter replied in a low, soft tone. His small bullet-coloured eyes were staring towards the edge of the town where the shacks were. The place where he had been able to find refuge from Fontaine's men whilst he recovered from his injuries. 'Got me a call to make first, then I'm headin' to Texas!'

'Why Texas?' Carmichael enquired.

Iron Eyes glanced at the large man. A hint of a smile etched his face. 'They got a whole lotta wanted men in Texas! Always good killin' to be had in Texas!'

The three figures watched the bounty hunter jab his spurs into the flesh of the grey. The horse responded and started to canter down the long street before Iron Eyes turned the animal and headed up behind the buildings to where the less wealthy townspeople lived.

Iron Eyes reined in and stared at the shack. Smoke still curled from its small chimney stack. The ill-fitting door opened and the small elderly female tried to see with eyes which no longer worked.

'Who is that? Speak up, boy?' Bessie Cooper said.

'Iron Eyes, Bessie!' the bounty hunter said.

'So ya still alive, huh?' She chuckled.

'Fontaine ain't, ma'am!' Iron Eyes informed her.

A smile traced across her face. Again, Iron Eyes could see the beauty she had once been. Age could not hide real beauty from eyes which saw far more than most.

'Ya killed him?'

'Yep!'

'Good!' The woman rested her hand on the door to aid her balance. 'Teddy's sleepin' on the bed. He only finished work a few hours back.'

'Don't wake him, Bessie.' Iron Eyes dismounted and opened the leather flap of the saddle-bag nearer to the shack. He hauled one of the hefty canvas sacks out of the satchel and carried it into the shack. He placed it down on the table. The legs of the table groaned under the weight.

'What ya got there, boy?' Bessie asked as she made her way to the tall man's side.

'Golden eagles, Bessie!' Iron Eyes whispered as he watched Ted snoring on the bed. 'A whole bunch of them.'

She did not understand.

'I ain't sure why ya brung that in here, boy.'

Iron Eyes walked back to the door. She held on to his arm and stopped his progress to his waiting mount. He turned and looked down at her. The white film which covered her pupils saddened him. Yet she appeared to see him better than most people who were unable to look beyond his brutal scars.

'Bounty money, Bessie! It's half what I earned for killin' that bunch of vermin! All legal! Ya can buy yaself a better house and have plenty of money left over for you and Ted to have a nice life!'

'But why ya givin' it to us, boy?' she asked. 'It was you who done for Fontaine and his cronies, not us!'

Iron Eyes inhaled.

'Without you and Ted, I reckon I'd not have bin able to go after them critters at all, let alone get the better of them! The money's yours. Ya earned it!'

Bessie was about to speak when he leaned down and placed a kiss on her cheek. Her misty eyes could just make out the blurred image of the tall bounty hunter as he stepped into his stirrup and mounted the grey once more.

'Take care, boy!' she ordered waving her finger at him.

'I'll surely try, Bessie!' Iron Eyes nodded.

'Ya a good man, Iron Eyes!' she said as a tear trailed down her cheek. 'A darn good man!'

He spurred and rode off between the shacks.

Ted Cooper opened his eyes and looked through the open doorway to his mother.

'Who was that, Ma?' He yawned.

'Iron Eyes!' she sighed. 'That was our dear friend Iron Eyes, Teddy!'

We do hope that you have enjoyed reading this large print book.

Did you know that all of our titles are available for purchase?

We publish a wide range of high quality large print books including:
Romances, Mysteries, Classics
General Fiction
Non Fiction and Westerns

Special interest titles available in large print are:
The Little Oxford Dictionary
Music Book, Song Book
Hymn Book, Service Book

Also available from us courtesy of Oxford University Press:
Young Readers' Dictionary
(large print edition)
Young Readers' Thesaurus
(large print edition)

For further information or a free brochure, please contact us at:
Ulverscroft Large Print Books Ltd.,
The Green, Bradgate Road, Anstey,
Leicester, LE7 7FU, England.
Tel: (00 44) **0116 236 4325**
Fax: (00 44) **0116 234 0205**

Other titles in the
Linford Western Library:

THE DRIFTER'S REVENGE

Owen G. Irons

Travelling to Oregon, drifter Ryan had taken a job in the new railroad's Montana timber camp. But he fled when company men killed his friend Ben Comfrey over owed wages of seventy-four dollars fifty . . . Ryan knew that Ben's widow and son needed that money to get them through the winter — but when he confronted the railroad bosses, they tried to kill him too. Now, with a capable gun and vengeance in mind, Ryan was going to pursue it to the end of the line.

LAWMAN'S LAMENT

David Bingley

When Judge Jonathan B. Lacey is killed in an ambush in Big Springs County, Texas, his dying words to town marshal Dan Marden alter the course of Dan's life. Quitting his work as marshal, Dan embarks upon a hunt for Lacey's murderers, the outlaw Long John Verne and his gang. Then Dan's brother Vance becomes involved in running battles between towns, making Dan's task almost impossible. Now the ex-marshal must struggle to complete his quest.

THE DYING TREE

Edward Thomson

With the railroad pushing into Indian territory, the peace treaty between the Sioux and the white men is broken. Sioux warriors attack railroad surveyors and only Civil War veteran Mike Wilson escapes. Serving his own purposes, the railroad boss schemes for an Indian war, which triggers an explosive and violent reaction from the local tribes. Now there would be war lasting for many years, drenching the prairie grass with the blood of Indians and white men alike.

FURY AT TROON'S FERRY

Mark Bannerman

In the gathering darkness he strode purposefully up the empty street. The only sounds came from the saloon; men's raucous voices and the shrill laughter of women. His wife, Leah, had once said that nothing was achieved by violence . . . But now he was convinced that she was wrong, and his desire was to inflict vengeance. Before bullets started flying, as surely they must, would he be able to extract the truth from the man he sought . . . and despised?

THE LONG SEARCH

Alan Irwin

When Deputy Sheriff Cliff McLaine was brutally tortured and murdered by the notorious gang of outlaws led by Will Jordan, his lawman brother Brad McLaine quit his job to embark on a search for the killers. His pursuit took him to New Mexico Territory, to Texas and to the Indian Territory where the Jordan gang had gone into hiding. But would Brad's grit, tenacity and gun-handling experience be enough to bring a ruthless band of outlaws to justice?

GUNS ON THE WAHOO

George J. Prescott

Fargo Reilly arrives in the town of Verdad de Soleil, where rancher Lucas Carter, is tightening his stranglehold. Reilly seems like a harmless drifter, but after demonstrating his skill with a Colt on Carter's son and thrashing the hulking ranch foreman, things begin to change. In truth, Reilly is a federal marshal. Events take a tangled course and Reilly must use some double dealing and chicanery. Only then can he silence Carter and the guns on the Wahoo.